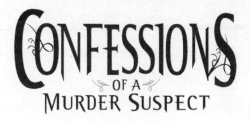

# CONFESSIONS
## OF A
## MURDER SUSPECT

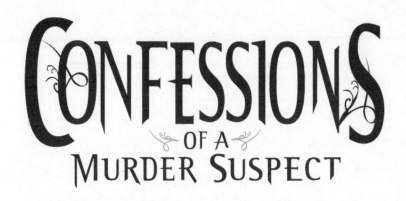

# James Patterson

## AND MAXINE PAETRO

Published by Young Arrow, 2012

2 4 6 8 10 9 7 5 3 1

First published in Great Britain in 2012 by
Young Arrow
Random House, 20 Vauxhall Bridge Road,
London SW1V 2SA

www.randomhouse.co.uk

Addresses for companies within The Random House Group Limited can be found at:
www.randomhouse.co.uk/offices.htm

The Random House Group Limited Reg. No. 954009

A CIP catalogue record for this book
is available from the British Library

Hardback ISBN 9780099567332
Trade paperback ISBN 9780099567349

The Random House Group Limited supports The Forest Stewardship Council
(FSC®), the leading international forest certification organisation. Our books carrying
the FSC label are printed on FSC® certified paper. FSC is the only forest certification
scheme endorsed by the leading environmental organisations,
including Greenpeace. Our paper procurement policy can be found at:
www.randomhouse.co.uk/environment

Printed in Great Britain by Clays Ltd, St Ives plc

TO THE CITY THAT NEVER SLEEPS, AND TO THE CITY
THAT GOES TO SLEEP AT EIGHT

# 1

# MURDER
## IN THE
## HOUSE OF ANGELS

*I have some really bad secrets* to share with someone, and it might as well be you—a stranger, a reader of books, but most of all, a person who can't hurt me. So here goes nothing, or maybe everything. I'm not sure if I can even tell the difference anymore.

The night my parents died—after they'd been carried out in slick black body bags through the service elevator—my brother Matthew shouted at the top of his powerful lungs, "My parents were vile, but they didn't deserve to be taken out with the *trash*!"

He was right about the last part—and, as things turned out, the first part as well.

But I'm getting ahead of myself, aren't I? Please forgive me....I do that a lot.

I'd been asleep downstairs, directly under my parents' bedroom, when it happened. So I never heard a thing—no frantic thumping, no terrified shouting, no fracas at all. I woke up to the scream of sirens speeding up Central Park West, maybe one of the most common sounds in New York City.

But that night it was different.

The sirens stopped *right downstairs*. That was what caused me to wake up with a hundred-miles-an-hour heartbeat. Was the building on fire? Did some old neighbor have a stroke?

I threw off my double layer of blankets, went to my window, and looked down to the street, nine dizzying floors below. I saw three police cruisers and what could have been an unmarked police car parked on Seventy-second Street, right at the front gates of our apartment building, the exclusive and infamous Dakota.

A moment later our intercom buzzed, a jarring *blat-blat* that punched right through my flesh and bones.

Why was the doorman paging *us*? This was *crazy*.

My bedroom was the one closest to the front door, so I bolted through the living room, hooked a right at the sharks in the aquarium coffee table, and passed between Robert and his nonstop TV.

When I reached the foyer, I stabbed at the intercom button to stop the irritating blare before it woke up the whole house.

I spoke in a loud whisper to the doorman through the speaker: "Sal? What's happening?"

"Miss Tandy? Two policemen are on the way up to your apartment right now. I couldn't stop them. They got a nine-one-one call. It's an emergency. That's what they said."

"There's been a mistake, Sal. Everyone is asleep here. It's after midnight. How could you let them up?"

Before Sal could answer, the doorbell rang, and then fists pounded the door. A harsh masculine voice called out, "This is the police."

I made sure the chain was in place and then opened the door—but just a crack.

I peered out through the opening and saw two men in the hallway. The older one was as big as a bear but kind of soft-looking and spongy. The younger one was wiry and had a sharp, expressionless face, something like a hatchet blade, or...no, a hatchet blade is exactly right.

The younger one flashed his badge and said, "Sergeant

Capricorn Caputo and Detective Ryan Hayes, NYPD. Please open the door."

*Capricorn Caputo?* I thought. *Seriously?* "You've got the wrong apartment," I said. "No one here called the police."

"Open the door, miss. And I mean *right now.*"

"I'll get my parents," I said through the crack. I had no idea that my parents were dead and that we would be the only serious suspects in a double homicide. I was in my last moment of innocence.

But who am I kidding? No one in the Angel family was ever innocent.

"*Open up*, or my partner will kick down the door!" Hatchet Face called out.

It is no exaggeration to say that my whole family was about to get a wake-up call from *hell*. But all I was thinking at that particular moment was that the police could *not* kick down the door. This was the *Dakota*. We could get *evicted* for allowing someone to disturb the peace.

I unlatched the chain and swung the door open. I was wearing pajamas, of course; chick-yellow ones with dinosaurs chasing butterflies. Not exactly what I would have chosen for a meeting with the police.

Detective Hayes, the bearish one, said, "What's your name?"

"Tandy Angel."

"Are you the daughter of Malcolm and Maud Angel?"

"I am. Can you please tell me why you're here?"

"Tandy is your real name?" he said, ignoring my question.

"I'm called Tandy. Please wait here. I'll get my parents to talk to you."

"We'll go with you," said Sergeant Caputo.

Caputo's grim expression told me that this was not a request. I turned on lights as we headed toward my parents' bedroom suite.

I was climbing the circular stairwell, thinking that my parents were going to kill me for bringing these men upstairs, when suddenly both cops pushed rudely past me. By the time I had reached my parents' room, the overhead light was on and the cops were bending over my parents' bed.

Even with Caputo and Hayes in the way, I could see that my mother and father looked all wrong. Their sheets and blankets were on the floor, and their nightclothes were bunched under their arms, as if they'd tried to take them off. My father's arm looked like it had been twisted out of its socket. My mother was lying facedown across my father's body, and her tongue was sticking out of her mouth. It had turned *black*.

I didn't need a coroner to tell me that they were dead. I knew it just moments after I saw them. Diagnosis certain.

I shrieked and ran toward them, but Hayes stopped me cold. He kept me out of the room, putting his big paws on my shoulders and forcibly walking me backward out to the hallway.

"I'm sorry to do this," he said, then shut the bedroom door in my face.

I didn't try to open it. I just stood there. Motionless. Almost not breathing.

So, you might be wondering why I wasn't bawling, screeching, or passing out from shock and horror. Or why I wasn't running to the bathroom to vomit or curling up in the fetal position, hugging my knees and sobbing. Or doing any of the things that a teenage girl who's just seen her murdered parents' bodies ought to do.

The answer is complicated, but here's the simplest way to say it: I'm not a whole lot like most girls. At least, not from what I can tell. For me, having a meltdown was seriously out of the question.

From the time I was two, when I first started speaking in paragraphs that began with topic sentences, Malcolm and Maud had told me that I was exceptionally smart. Later, they told me that I was analytical and focused, and that my detachment from watery emotion was a superb trait. They said that if I nurtured these qualities, I would achieve or even exceed my extraordinary potential, and this wasn't just a good thing, but a great thing. It was the only thing that mattered, in fact.

It was a challenge, and I had accepted it.

That's why I was more prepared for this catastrophe than most kids my age would be, or maybe *any* kids my age.

Yes, it was true that panic was shooting up and down my spine and zinging out to my fingertips. I was shocked, maybe even terrified. But I quickly tamped down the screaming voice inside my head and collected my wits, along with the few available facts.

One: My parents had died in some unspeakable way.

Two: Someone had known about their deaths and called the police.

Three: Our doors were locked, and there had been no obvious break-in. Aside from me, my brothers Harry and Hugo and my mother's personal assistant, Samantha, were the only ones home.

I went downstairs and got my phone. I called both my uncle Peter and our lawyer, Philippe Montaigne. Then I went to each of my siblings' bedrooms, and to Samantha's, too. And somehow, I told them each the inexpressibly horrible news that our mother and father were dead, and that it was possible they'd been murdered.

*Can you imagine the words you'd use,* dear reader, to tell your family that your parents had been murdered? I hope so, because I'm not going to be able to share those wretched moments with you right now. We're just getting to know each other, and I take a little bit of time to warm up to people. Can you be patient with me? I promise it'll be worth the wait.

After I'd completed that horrible task—perhaps the worst task of my life—I tried to focus my fractured attention back on Sergeant Capricorn Caputo. He was a rough-looking character, like a bad cop in a black-and-white film from the forties who smoked unfiltered cigarettes, had stained fingers, and was coughing up his lungs on his way to the cemetery.

Caputo looked to be about thirty-five years old. He had one continuous eyebrow, a furry ledge over his stony black eyes. His thin lips were set in a short, hard line. He had rolled up the sleeves of his shiny blue jacket, and I noted a zodiac sign tattooed on his wrist.

He looked like *exactly* the kind of detective I wanted to have working on the case of my murdered parents.

Gnarly and mean.

Detective Hayes was an entirely different cat. He had a basically pleasant, faintly lined face and wore a wedding ring, an NYPD Windbreaker, and steel-tipped boots. He looked sympathetic to us kids, sitting in a stunned semi-circle around him. But Detective Hayes wasn't in charge, and he wasn't doing the talking.

Caputo stood with his back to our massive fireplace and coughed into his fist. Then he looked around the living room with his mouth wide open.

He couldn't believe how we lived.

And I can't say I blame him.

He took in the eight-hundred-gallon aquarium coffee table with the four glowing pygmy sharks swimming circles around their bubbler.

His jaw dropped even farther when he saw the life-size merman hanging by its tail from a bloody hook and chain in the ceiling near the staircase.

He sent a glance across the white-lacquered grand piano, which we called "Pegasus" because it looked like it had wings.

And he stared at Robert, who was slumped over in a La-Z-Boy with a can of Bud in one hand and a remote control in the other, just watching the static on his TV screen.

Robert is a remarkable creation. He really is. It's next to impossible to tell that he, his La-Z-Boy, and his very own TV are all part of an incredibly lifelike, technologically advanced sculpture. He was cast from a real person, then rendered in polyvinyl and an auto-body filler composite called Bondo. Robert looks so real, you half expect him to crunch his beer can against his forehead and ask for another cold one.

"What's the point of this thing?" Detective Caputo asked.

"It's an artistic style called hyperrealism," I responded.

"Hyper-real, huh?" Detective Caputo said. "Does that mean 'over-the-top'? Because that's kind of a theme in this family, isn't it?"

No one answered him. To us, this was home.

When Detective Caputo was through taking in the décor, he fixed his eyes on each of us in turn. We just blinked at him. There were no hysterics. In fact, there was no apparent emotion at all.

"Your parents were *murdered*," he said. "Do you get that? What's the matter? No one here loved them?"

We did love them, but it wasn't a simple love. To start with, my parents were complicated: strict, generous, punishing, expansive, withholding. And as a result, we were complicated, too. I knew all of us felt what I was feeling—an internal tsunami of horror and loss and confusion. But we couldn't show it. Not even to save our lives.

Of course, Sergeant Caputo didn't see us as bereaved children going through the worst day of our tender young lives. He saw us as *suspects*, every one of us a "person of interest" in a locked-door double homicide.

He didn't try to hide his judgment, and I couldn't fault his reasoning.

I thought he was right.

My parents' killer was in that room.

My gaze *turned to the angry face* of my ten-year-old "little" brother, Hugo. From the look of outrage he directed toward the cops, I got the feeling that he felt they were villains, and that he wanted to take Sergeant Caputo apart like a rotisserie chicken. The thing is, Hugo is probably as strong as a full-grown man. I thought he could actually do it.

What else could Hugo do?

He sat in the "Pork Chair," a pink upholstered armchair with carved wooden pig hooves for feet. He looked adorable, as he almost always did. He was wearing an enormous Giants sweatshirt over his pajamas. Because Goliath was his biblical hero, he allowed a haircut only once a year, so it had been eleven months since Hugo's last trim and his brown hair eddied down his back like a mountain stream.

My twin brother, Harrison—aka Harry—sat on the red leather sofa across from Hugo. You would like Harry; everyone does. We're fraternal twins, of course, but we look very much alike, with dark eyes and hair that we got from our mother. I wear my hair below my shoulders, sometimes with a headband. Harry's hair has curls that I would die for. He wears Harry Potter–style dark-rimmed glasses. We both twirl our hair with our fingers when deep in thought. I do it clockwise, and he does it in the other direction.

Harry also has a great smile. I guess I do, too, but I almost never use it. Harry uses his a lot. Maybe he's the only Angel who does, actually.

That night, Harry wore painter's pants and a sweatshirt with the hood pulled half over his face, which told me that he wanted to disappear. His breathing sounded wheezy, like he had a harmonica in his throat, which meant an asthma attack was coming on.

Samantha Peck, my mother's kind and beautiful live-in personal assistant, had spent the night in the apartment, behind our locked doors. She worked for Maud, and that made her a suspect, too. She stood behind Hugo with her hand on his shoulder, her sandy-colored braid cascading over her pink satin robe. Her face was drawn and pale, as if her heart had stopped pumping. I thought she might be in shock.

Caputo pointed at Robert's TV, which broadcast static 24/7. He said, "Can someone turn that off?"

Hugo said, "We never turn it off. Never."

Caputo walked to the wall and pulled the plug.

For an instant, the room was completely quiet, as Caputo watched us to see how we would react. I found myself wishing more than anything that my older brother, Matthew, would suddenly appear. I had tried to reach him several times, but he wasn't answering his phone. He may not have been on the best terms with our parents, but I wouldn't be able to entirely focus until he had been informed of their deaths. And Matthew, I was sure, would know how to deal with these police officers.

Sergeant Caputo shoved his sleeves up farther on his forearms and said, "The penthouse is a crime scene. It's off-limits until I say otherwise. Are we all clear?"

I thought about how my parents would have wanted us to behave in this situation.

My mother was like a perpetual-motion machine, never stopping, hardly sleeping at all. She seemed to barely notice people—even her children. Her strength was in analyzing financial markets and managing the billions in her exclusive hedge fund.

My father co-owned Angel Pharmaceuticals with his younger brother, Peter. He was a chemist with a gigantic brain and enormous gifts. Unlike my mother, Malcolm engaged with us so intensely that after a few minutes of contact with my father, I felt invaded to the core.

Even with all their faults, Malcolm and Maud had had their children's interests at heart. They tirelessly taught us to harness what they called our "superhuman powers": our physical strengths, our emotions, and our remarkable IQs.

Our parents wanted us to be perfect.

Even in this situation, they would've wanted us to behave perfectly.

You can probably imagine that the constant press toward perfection might affect your relationships with others and the expectations you have of yourself. It's like being a camera and the subject of its photographs at the same time.

That's screwed up, right?

Still, somehow the Angel kids survived this—perhaps by a means that I might describe as . . . *not entirely natural.* But we'll get to that later.

For the moment, I decided to use the skills my parents

had driven into all of us, and to refuse to react the way Caputo wanted me to.

"Of course, Officer Caputo," I finally responded to his demand. "We wouldn't want to interfere in your very thorough investigation."

I would just have to wait until the officers were out of my way.

# CONFESSION

*If only Caputo could interrogate Robert.* You see, Robert sees stuff. He *knows* stuff. About the Angels. About me.

Such as: He knows about the time I put my foot right through his TV screen.

*On purpose.* Or so I'm told.

I don't even remember it. But I know it happened because one day I was the best lacrosse player at All Saints, and the next day I woke up in the hospital with fifty stitches in my foot and leg.

In the hospital, Malcolm's and Maud's stern faces had looked at me without sympathy. Maud said she never thought lacrosse was good for me, anyway. (I would never play again.) Malcolm announced that my Big Chop was going to be repairing Robert so that he was as good as new. (My efforts were, sadly, flawed; that's why Robert only watches static these days.)

And that's pretty much all they'd told me. You don't demand answers from Malcolm and Maud.

Hugo was the only one who saw what happened. He said I flew into the apartment in such a rage that he hid behind the Claes Oldenburg sculpture and watched me kick the hell out of Robert, screaming, *"They killed her. They killed her!"* My foot crashed through Robert's screen with the force of a wrecking ball, he claims.

How could I do that? I'd need almost superhuman strength. When I asked Matthew, he shrugged and said only: "It's a piece of art, Tandy. It's not industrial strength."

More important, though, was *why* I would do that. Could I really have been talking about my dead sister, Katherine?

Was I accusing Malcolm and Maud of killing their eldest daughter?

*And why don't I remember it at all?*

Caputo was still pacing and coughing, giving us the evil eye and warning us that if we crossed into the no-go zone of the penthouse suite, he would have us removed from the apartment.

"I'm doing you a favor, letting you stay downstairs. Don't make me sorry."

I stared back at the menacing detective and remembered what it had been like growing up here in the Dakota—a gated island on an island. It was one of the few places in the world where I felt secure.

Yet Malcolm and Maud Angel weren't the first people to be killed at the Dakota. Everyone knows that Mark David Chapman gunned John Lennon down right at the front gates, where the police cars were now parked. And just two floors below us, the actor Gig Young killed his wife and then shot himself.

Now my parents had been murdered in their own bed by an unknown killer for a reason I couldn't imagine.

Or maybe I could...but I digress. Those are very private thoughts, for later.

As I sat beside Harry, under the withering gaze of Sergeant Caputo, crime-scene investigators trooped through the private entranceway that very few New Yorkers had ever seen, even in photographs. They crossed the cobbled courtyard and used the residents' elevators to come upstairs, which was strictly forbidden by the cooperative's bylaws.

Sergeant Caputo had banned us from our parents' suite—but I *lived* there. I had rights. And I had already taught myself basic criminology.

I learned all about JonBenét Ramsey when I was six, the same age she'd been when she was murdered. She had been an adorable little girl, seemingly happy and unafraid and loving. I was so moved by her death that I wrote to the police in Colorado, asking them why they hadn't found her killer. No one wrote back. To this day, her killer has not been found.

The unsolved Ramsey case had inspired me to read

up on the famous forensic pathologists Michael Baden and Henry Lee. I had consumed practical guides to homicide investigations, so I knew that the longer it took to solve a crime, the more likely it was that it would never be solved.

I wasn't one to trust authority. Who knows, though— maybe Caputo and Hayes *were* decent cops. But my parents were just a case to them. That was all they could ever be.

Malcolm and Maud were my *parents*. I owed them. I owed it to myself, and to my siblings, to try to solve their murders.

The fact is, I was the ideal detective for this case. This was a job that I could—and *should*—do. Please don't think I'm completely full of myself when I say that. I just knew that my doggedness and personal motivation would trump any training these guys had.

I am an Angel, after all. As Malcolm always said, we get things done.

So as I sat in the living room that night, I took on the full responsibility of finding my parents' killer—even if it turned out that the killer shared my DNA.

Even if it turned out to be me.

You shouldn't count that out, friend.

*Are you familiar with the phrase* unreliable narrator? Maybe from English-lit class? It's when the storyteller might not be worthy of your trust. In fact, the storyteller might be a complete liar. So given what I just said, you're probably wondering: Is that me?

Would I do that to you? Of course I wouldn't. At least, I don't think I would. But you can never tell about people, can you? How much do you really know about my past?

That's a subject we'll have to investigate together, later.

For now, back to my story. I was about to begin the investigation of my parents' murders. While the two detectives conferred in the study, out of sight, I climbed the stairs to the long hallway in my parents' penthouse suite. I flattened myself against the dark red wall and averted my eyes as the techs from the medical examiner's office took my parents away in body bags.

Then I edged down the hall to the threshold of Malcolm and Maud's bedroom and peered inside.

An efficient-looking crime-scene investigator was busily dusting for fingerprints. The name tag on her shirt read CSI JOYCE YEAGER.

I said hello to the freckle-faced CSI and told her my name. She said that she was sorry for my loss. I nodded, then said, "Do you mind if I ask you some questions?"

CSI Yeager looked around before saying, "Okay."

I didn't have time for tact. I'd been warned away from this room and everything in it, so I began to shoot questions at the CSI as if I were firing them from a nail gun.

"What was the time of death?"

"That hasn't been determined," she said.

"And the means?"

"We don't know yet how your parents were killed."

"And what about the manner of death?" I asked.

"The medical examiner will determine if these were homicides, accidents, natural deaths—"

"Natural?" I interrupted, already getting fed up. "Come on."

"It's the medical examiner's job to determine these things," she said.

"Have you found a weapon? Was there any blood?"

"Listen, Tandy. I'm sorry, but you have to go now, before you get me in trouble."

CSI Yeager was ignoring me now, but she didn't close the door. I looked around the room, taking in the enormous four-poster bed and the silk bedspread on the floor.

And I did a visual inventory of my parents' valuables.

The painting over their fireplace, by Daniel Aronstein, was a modern depiction of an American flag: strips of frayed muslin layered with oil paints in greens and mauve. It was worth almost $200,000—and it hadn't been touched.

My mother's expensive jewelry was also untouched; her strand of impossibly creamy Mikimoto pearls lay in an open velvet-lined box on the dresser, and her twelve-carat emerald ring still hung from a branch of the crystal ring tree beside her bed.

It could not be clearer that there had been no robbery here.

It shouldn't surprise me that the evidence pointed to the fact that my parents had been killed out of anger, fear, hatred…

Or revenge.

As I stood outside my parents' bedroom a shadow fell across me and I jumped, as if I were already living in fear of the ghosts of Malcolm and Maud. Many ghosts in my family already haunt us, friend, so it helps me to know that you're here.

Fortunately, this shadow just belonged to Sergeant Caputo. He pinched my shoulder. Hard.

"Let's go, Tansy. I told you, this floor is off-limits. Entering a crime scene before it's cleared is evidence tampering. It's against the law."

"Tandy," I said. "Not Tansy. Tandy."

I didn't argue his point; he was right. Instead, I went ahead of him down the stairs and back to the living room, arriving just as my big brother, Matthew, stormed in from the kitchen.

When Matthew entered a room, he seemed to draw all the light and air to him. He had light brown dreadlocks tied in a bunch with a hank of yarn, and intense blue eyes that shone like high beams.

I've never seen eyes like his. No one has.

Matty was dressed in jeans and a black T-shirt under a leather jacket, but anyone would've sworn he was wearing a bodysuit with an emblem on the chest and a cape fluttering behind.

Hugo broke the spell by leaping out of his chair. "Hup!" he yelled at Matty, jumping toward his brother with outstretched arms.

Matthew caught Hugo easily and put a hand to the back of his baby brother's head while fastening his eyes on the two homicide detectives.

Matthew is six-two and has biceps the size of thighs. And, well, he can be a little scary when he's mad.

*Mad* wasn't even the word to describe him that night.

"*My parents* were just carried out of the building in the *service* elevator," he shouted at the cops. "They were *vile*, but they didn't deserve to be taken out with the *trash*!"

Detective Hayes said, "And you are...?"

"Matthew Angel. Malcolm and Maud's son."

"And how did you get into the apartment?" Hayes said.

"Cops let me in. One of them wanted my autograph."

Caputo said to Matthew, "You won the Heisman last year, right?"

Matthew nodded. In addition to having won the Heisman and being a three-time all-American, Matthew was a poster boy for the NFL and had a fat Nike contract. The sportscaster Aran Delaney had once said of Matthew's blazing speed and agility, "He can run around the block between the time I strike a match and light my cigarette. Matthew Angel is not just a cut above, but an order of *magnitude* above other outstanding athletes." So it didn't surprise me that Caputo recognized my brother.

Matty was sneering, as if the mention of his celebrity was offensive under the circumstances. I kind of had to agree. *Who cares about his stupid Heisman right now?*

Fortunately, Hayes was all business. "Look, Matthew. I'm sorry we had to take your folks out the back way. You wouldn't have wanted them carried around the front so the rubberneckers could gawk and take pictures, would you? Please sit down. We have a few questions."

"I'll stand," Matthew said. By that point, Hugo had climbed around Matthew's body and was on his back, looking at the cops over his brother's shoulder.

Caputo went right into hostility mode. "Where have you been for the last six hours?"

"I stayed with my girlfriend on West Ninth Street. We were together all night, and she'll be happy to tell you that."

Matthew's girlfriend was the actress Tamara Gee. She'd received an Academy Award nomination the previous year, when she was twenty-three, and was almost as famous as Matty. I should have realized he would be at her apartment, but I really had no way of contacting him there. I met Tamara the one time Matty brought her home to meet our parents, and while she was certainly pretty in real life, and maybe an order of *magnitude* above other actors in smarts, I understood easily from her posture and way of speaking that she wanted nothing to do with us. She certainly wasn't passing out her phone number in case I ever needed to call my brother at her apartment. Especially in the dead of night, to inform him that our parents had been murdered.

My father, on the other hand, seemed to admire Tamara's obvious distrust of us, and later remarked to me that she was the last piece of the puzzle to make Matthew's future all but certain. You see, he wanted Matty to run for president one day. He was certain Matty would win.

Incidentally, Malcolm also thought that Matthew was a sociopath. But, except for Harry, all of us, including my father, had been called sociopaths at some time in our lives.

"My siblings will tell you that I haven't set foot in this place, or even seen my parents, for months," Matthew was saying to Detective Hayes.

"You have a problem with your parents?" Hayes asked.

"I'm twenty-four. I've flown the coop." Matthew didn't even try to disguise the fact that he had no use for Malcolm and Maud.

"We'll check out your alibi soon enough," Caputo snapped. "But listen: We all know you could have left your girlfriend in the Village, killed your parents, and gone back to bed before your twinkie even knew you were gone."

It was just short of an accusation, obviously meant to provoke a reaction from Matthew. But my big brother didn't bite. Instead, he turned to Hugo and said, "I'm going to tuck you into bed, Buddy."

Caputo hadn't gotten anything from Matty, but he'd forced me to face my own suspicions. My brother hated our parents. He was a 215-pound professional football player, a cunning brute.

Was he also a killer?

# CONFESSION

*I have pretty bad associations* with the Heisman. My therapist, Dr. Keyes, has done a lot to help me forget that night, but every now and then, a memory will pierce my mind's eye.

It was after the celebration, after we'd returned to the apartment from dinner at Le Cirque. Malcolm and Matty had both had more than a few drinks at that point, and Malcolm said, "So, let me hold the Angel family Heisman now, son." He latched on to the trophy, like Matty should hand it over. "Remember, you owe everything to us," he went on. "Your speed, your strength, your endurance. Your career. Your money."

That did not go over well with Matty. To say the least.

"I didn't *ask* for what you gave me," he said through clenched teeth. He slammed his fist on the glass dining table and I jumped as a crack appeared, sure his fist was going to get sliced to ribbons. Matty was so angry I don't think he would have even noticed. "You created each and every one of us to live out one of your *freakish childhood fantasies*! We're Malcolm's puppets. Maud's baby dolls. Malcolm and Maud's *precious little trophies*."

And that's when he hurled the Heisman trophy through the living room window, less than two inches above my head.

He could have killed someone walking down below. He could have killed *me*. Would he have regretted it?

They didn't call us sociopaths for nothing.

*Now that I've told you that memory,* I've got to get it out of my head, and quick. That's one thing you should know about me: My head is a strange—and maybe a little dangerous—place to be for too long. So I'm just going to give you little bits and pieces at a time. Because I want you to like me; I need a friend. Someone willing to be right here with me and feel the horror of the night my parents died. Can you do that for me?

I could feel the floorboards shaking as Matthew stormed out of the room, but Sergeant Caputo wasn't intimidated. He barked at the rest of us, still sitting around the fireplace, "Who was the last person to see Mr. and Mrs. Angel alive?"

It was a fair question, and I considered the possibilities. Samantha, my mother's live-in assistant, went off-duty at six. She hadn't been invited to the dinner that had been served in our dining room at eight, for my parents' guest, the ambassador from the Kingdom of Bhutan.

Hugo had also been excluded from our dinner with the ambassador and had gone to his bedroom at seven.

Harry and I had been at the table for the entire spectacle, and when it was over, Harry had gone to his room and, as usual, locked the door.

My parents had shown the ambassador to the elevator, and when I last saw them, in the study an hour later, they were in perfect form. Maud was poised elegantly on the edge of her favorite leather chair, and I saw that she had changed out of her silk pantsuit and into one of her favorite embroidered Tunisian tunics. My father was sitting in his own leather chair, sipping his customary glass of scotch. Neither of them looked even the slightest bit agitated.

In answer to Caputo's question, Samantha, who had taken over Hugo's seat in the Pork Chair, said, "I saw them last. Maud texted me about some documents in need of signatures, so I reported to her at eleven thirty." Her voice wobbled the smallest bit when she said Maud's name, but hearing her familiar, gentle voice calmed me slightly.

"How did she seem to you?"

"Perfectly Maud," said Samantha.

"What does that mean?" Caputo followed up. He wasn't about to use his imagination.

Samantha brushed a loose lock of sandy hair out of her eyes and stared at Caputo. "It means exactly that. *Perfect.* Not a hair out of place, not a worry line to be found. Calm. Collected. Ready to take on whatever came next."

Caputo dismissed this and barreled ahead. "Who stands to profit from the deaths of these people?"

Samantha deflected the question. "Please remember that I'm having a hard time right now," she said, the wobble returning to her voice. "I loved *these people* and am still in shock that they've been ripped from our lives forever."

I thought I understood what Caputo was doing. When murder suspects are stressed, they sometimes make mistakes and tell the cops a story that might later become evidence against them.

Caputo asked again, "Miss Peck. Who stood to profit from the deaths of Mr. and Mrs. Angel?"

"I couldn't say."

"Can't say or won't say?"

"I don't *know*," Samantha said. "I can't imagine someone could want them dead. They may have had some… unorthodox quirks, but they were good people."

Between coughing fits, Caputo grilled her on her where-abouts that evening and got information on the friend Samantha had gone to dinner with at Carmine's Trattoria on the West Side. He asked about her relationships with all of us, to which she responded succinctly that while Maud was her employer, each of us kids was like family to her. She had been a part of our lives for years, initially as the photog-rapher who took our family portraits—she'd taken hun-dreds of beautiful photographs of the family over the years, many of which were hung around the apartment, equal to the Leibovitz portraits we owned—and then, after proving her ability to be totally discreet and loyal, as Maud's personal secretary. I couldn't remember a time when she wasn't with us, and as she told Caputo, she would do anything for us.

When Caputo was finished jotting down everything Samantha had to say, he turned his narrow, peevish eyes to Harry.

Harry was openmouthed and breathing thickly, leaning against me, sitting as close as if we were still nestled together in the womb.

"How come you're the only Angel kid who seems upset?" Caputo said to Harry.

"I'm…damaged," he said, quoting what Malcolm had said to him many times. "My emotions are getting the best of me. I'm sorry."

"Do you want to tell me something, Harrington?" Caputo said, putting his face inches from Harry's nose. "What do you want to tell me?"

"What do you want me to say? I hurt all over," Harry cried, "inside and out. This is absolutely the worst thing that has ever happened to me!" I put my arms around Harry and he burst into tears against my chest.

Nice-guy Hayes took it upon himself to step in with a smile and a "there, there" for Harry. I could tell without a doubt that he was about to give us the good-cop routine.

And I would be ready for it.

9

"*Do you want to go to your room,* Harry?" Hayes asked. Harry nodded vigorously. "Go ahead. I'll stop in and talk to you privately in a few minutes."

Harry shot out of his seat and ran to his room, bawling like a baby. Caputo looked dumbfounded, like he'd never seen a teenager cry before. Which was strange, because just minutes earlier he had been acting like we were all murderers for *not* crying our eyes out.

After a moment passed, Detective Hayes sat next to me on the red leather sofa. "Tandy, tell me your movements of the last six hours. We have to do a complete report, you understand. It's necessary for us to know where everyone was when your folks were killed."

"They weren't *folks*," I said. "Trust me on that."

I sketched the details of my evening for the detective, telling him about my homework and the time I'd spent doing research on the effects of radiation on shellfish in the Pacific. I talked about dinner, but mostly just to say that my father, an expert cook, had made the meal himself. I had watched. He had been teaching me how to cook, although I had yet to be allowed to touch anything he was going to serve. "Watch me and learn my movements to perfection so that when you first attempt to do it, you can't fail," he'd said.

I was about to give Detective Hayes the ambassador's name and number when his phone rang and he excused himself. When he returned, he asked me, "And how did your parents seem at dinner?"

I had thought Maud seemed a little off, maybe preoccupied, but I didn't say so. I also skipped over any mention of the ambassador, and I felt fine about the omission. I'd been in the same room with the ambassador every minute that he was in our house, and besides, that overstuffed, freeloading bureaucrat was too self-involved to ever commit murder.

I had just made a mistake I would pay for later.

"The food was excellent, as usual, and we all had a good time at dinner," I told Hayes. "I said good night to them before I went to bed at eleven."

"Your bedroom is right under theirs," Hayes said. "Did you hear any strange sounds, anything we should know about, Tandy?"

He was working me softly, trying to get to me to open up, but I had nothing for him. I had nothing for my own investigation, either.

I said, "I was asleep by eleven fifteen. And I sleep like a stump."

"How does a stump sleep?" Hayes asked with a smile.

He was patronizing me. To be fair, sometimes I look younger than I am. I've got small bones and features. I rarely use makeup. Girls' size-eight clothing fits me. As a result, people often underestimate me—which is how I like it.

"I sleep deeply," I said, "but my brain works overtime, organizing everything I've learned during the day," I told him. "I do some very good work in my sleep."

Hayes said, "All right, Tandy. Duly noted. *Works in her sleep.*"

He had run out of questions for me, but I had a few questions for him. And as long as he answered them, I didn't care if he patted me on the head while he did it. It takes a lot to set me off; I've been thoroughly trained to control my emotions.

"As far as I could tell, Detective Hayes, no gun or other

murder weapon was found. There was also no forced entry into the apartment. Valuables are still in my parents' room: a two-hundred-thousand-dollar work of art and several pieces of jewelry. This wasn't a robbery, correct?" I said. "So what is your theory of the crime?"

Sergeant Caputo had been watching Hayes interrogate me, and he was not amused. He certainly didn't want to cede control to a teenage girl wearing dinosaur pajamas.

Caputo bent so close to me, I could count the hairs in his unibrow, and the ones curling out of his nose, too.

"Tessie, I think you know a lot more about what happened to your parents than you want to say. Help us understand what happened here. Take a deep breath and tell us what you know. The truth feels really good when you just let it go."

I pulled back and said, "I *told* you the truth. I was sleeping. Like a stump. And I didn't wake up until I heard sirens. After that, you were pounding on the door."

I flashed what Harry calls my Anne Hathaway smile at the cops and said, "Thank you for your help in our time of need."

"Are we being dismissed?" asked Detective Hayes.

"Ah, finally, the right question," I replied.

"And the answer to that question is no," Caputo said.

"We'll go when we're done, and for your information, Child Protective Services is on the way."

Samantha jumped up then. "Mr. and Mrs. Angel elected Peter Angel to be the children's guardian in case of an emergency. Peter just texted me to say that he'll be here shortly."

Uncle Peter? Despite the fact that he was now our closest living relative, he was the last person I wanted to see—a busybody who had once proved to me he was not to be trusted. But that's a story for another time.

# 10

*Have you noticed* that time seems to slow down unbelievably during any emergency situation? Maybe not. I'm sorry to say this isn't the first emergency situation I've ever been in. So I knew this feeling of eternity all too well.

Though it felt like an hour, only about ten minutes passed before I found myself opening the front door to Uncle Peter, who stalked in like he owned the place. He was wearing a rumpled plaid suit, and his wispy hair had been finger-combed and wouldn't lie down. It looked to me like he'd been drinking.

He didn't quite meet my eyes when he said, "This is sad, Tandy. I'm sorry to hear the news."

I thought I could get more sympathy from a stranger on the street, but never mind. Peter was an Angel, after all.

"It's sad, all right," I said to my uncle, successfully quelling the wave of grief that surged up from my heart.

Directly behind him stood Philippe Montaigne, our family's attorney. We'd known Phil since we were young; he was actually Hugo's godfather.

He looked handsome and impeccable, even at three in the morning. His hair was shaved close to his scalp, and he smelled of Vetiver. His jacket was Armani, and he wore a white shirt that was open at the neck and hanging out over his dark trousers.

He held out his arms to me and I went to him for a hug. He said, "I'm sorry, Tandy. So very sorry. Are you all right? Do you know what happened?"

I whispered against his cheek, "No. And the police are clueless, Phil."

Uncle Peter conferred with Hayes and Caputo, and I heard him say that he had hosted a dinner party at his apartment from eight PM until only moments ago, and that he had eighteen guests who could vouch for his whereabouts.

As Hayes took down names and phone numbers, I brought Philippe up to the minute on everything I knew.

"All right. Now, don't talk to the police again unless I'm with you, Tandy."

"We only said that we were sleeping when it happened."

"That's fine," said Philippe. "Keep in mind that the police are allowed to lie. They can say anything to you. Set any kind of trap."

"Gotcha," I said.

"Good. And don't worry."

But it looked as if our fifteen-hundred-dollars-an-hour attorney was worried himself. I could tell he was wondering what would happen to us, the superfreak Angel kids, without the protection of our gargoyle parents.

Philippe approached the cops and I followed right behind him. "Is anyone here under arrest?" he asked.

"Not yet," said Caputo. "But we haven't excluded anyone as a suspect, either."

"Tandoori, Harrison, and Hugo are all minors. You had no right to interrogate them without a parent or guardian *ad litem* present."

"Their parents had checked out, for Christ's sake," Caputo said. "They could be witnesses to a double homicide. You think I should have made them hot chocolate and told them to watch cartoons? We had dead people here."

Phil ignored him and kept going.

"I'm going to file a complaint with the chief of Ds in the morning. Right now, I'm advising my clients not to speak with you unless you charge them, and even then only if I'm present. I'm also advising them all to go to bed. That includes Matthew, if he wants to stay, and Samantha Peck, too."

Caputo said, "The Angels' bedroom is a crime scene. We're leaving uniformed officers at the top of the stairs. I wouldn't mess with us if I were you, counselor. Be advised of *that*."

And with that, Caputo and Hayes finally left our apartment.

Uncle Peter stood in the center of the room, watching and saying nothing. He hadn't hugged me, or asked where my three brothers were so he could go to see them. He's made no secret of the fact that he doesn't like children.

He especially doesn't like us.

Why, you might ask?

*Because*, he has said, *I know you.*

He looked around the apartment as if he were sizing it up for sale. I knew for a fact that the apartment could fetch twenty million, and that was without the art and the fur-nishings. Uncle Peter would probably get my father's half of Angel Pharma, but would he inherit our apartment as well?

Uncle Peter said to me, "I'm moving into the guest room

for now. After the reading of the will, we'll see what the future will bring to the Angel family."

My jaw dropped. We didn't *have* a "guest room." And that could only mean one thing.

I watched as Uncle Peter went into the bedroom right next to mine. Oh, man, I could *not* believe it. If my parents had been alive, they might have killed Peter for using Katherine's room.

And I'm not exactly using *kill* as a figure of speech here.

# CONFESSION

*I saw Maud cry once.*

I know you probably don't believe that's possible, but it's true. I need to prove to you that my parents really were human. That they could feel pain.

I can't place the memory specifically in time; I imagine this is one of those traumatic moments that Dr. Keyes worked so hard to help me forget, but somehow it still lingers.

I remember that I'd come home early that day because lacrosse practice had been canceled unexpectedly. So I know it was before the accident with Robert that landed me in the hospital with fifty stitches.

As I entered the apartment, I heard a strange, strangled noise coming from the direction of Maud's study.

Others might have sprinted toward the sound to make sure there was no foul play, or maybe called out, asking if everyone was all right. But I think I'm a born investigator. When I hear something unusual, it's my nature to get quiet and observe, to study. So I took my shoes off, the Angel family rule, and padded quietly down the hall.

When I reached the door to the study, which was cracked open, I heard Samantha's voice. "Of course you had to do it. A mother's role is to prepare and protect her child. Period. You knew what he would do to her."

There was brief silence, then a gasp, then a wail. "We did something much worse, Samantha." It was Maud's voice, twisted with emotion. "What we did...the consequences are final. I have never failed so spectacularly in my life."

"You didn't fail. The person who you hired to do the job failed."

"I shouldn't have trusted him."

"But it was an accident."

"Accidents are the very definition of failure. Pure, complete failure."

"Maud, the past can't be changed. You can only let yourself think of the future. Of what's next. Let's discuss what can be done to...clean up. Let's discuss how I can help."

"Malcolm is taking care of that part. The person who did this will be taken care of. Permanently."

Permanently taken care of? *Fired*, I reassured myself. *That must be what she means.*

The person who did…what? Were they talking about someone working for the hedge fund? Or the man driving the vehicle that had killed Katherine?

Or the boy who had tried to steal their precious Tandoori away from them?

The boy I think I loved…once?

I'm so sorry, reader. I can't go on thinking about that right now.

# 11

*Our apartment suddenly felt completely empty.*

The police were gone, except for the oversized and overweight patrolman putting great stress on an antique armchair outside our parents' room.

The CSIs were gone.

Hugo had, for obvious reasons, not been able to sleep, and had followed Matty back to the living room. He was now quietly feeding squid-burger to the sharks while Matty paced. Harry had also returned from his room and was sitting at the piano with his head in his hands.

Philippe Montaigne was gone, and Uncle Peter had shut himself up in Katherine's room and locked the door. Shortly after the sounds of furniture being moved had ceased, the bar of light showing under the door had also gone out.

And, of course, our parents were gone. They'd left a gigantic vacuum. I never realized until that moment how much they'd filled this apartment. Our world. With all the silence around us, I wondered for a moment if they had been the Angel family's entire life force.

Matthew shattered the silence by whistling loudly, shrilly, and long.

"Attention, everyone," he shouted, putting on his sunglasses. "It's time for a family meeting, and Samantha is invited to attend."

Matty had our attention. Harry sat up at the Pegasus, his fingers on the keys. Samantha and I shared the sofa, and Hugo lay on the carpet with a couple of forty-pound weights in his hands. He curled them to his chest as his idol and mentor talked.

"Here's the thing, sports fans, and you, too, Tandy. United we stand. Divided we fall. Don't talk to the police without Philippe. Don't speculate on what could have happened, or why. That only muddies the waters. Let the police do their work. We stand on the sidelines." He slid his sunglasses down his nose and looked around the room at us. "Anybody have anything to add to this?"

Well, yeah. *I* did.

"Matty, it's obvious that we're all suspects," I said. "The police didn't believe our alibis, and why should they? No one else had access to the apartment. The doors lock automatically. The elevator requires a key. It's pretty clear to them that one of us murdered Maud and Malcolm."

"That's what I'm talking about, Tandy, that's the exact thing. They don't know if it was one of us. Maybe you gave a key to a boyfriend—"

"You know I don't have a boyfriend." That was cruel on Matty's part. He knew we did not speak about boyfriends in this house. At least mine... Because they weren't allowed.

This, dear friend, was the paradox of my life. Even though I'd traveled the world—more than once—you might say I didn't get out much. At all.

Matty was still talking. "Or maybe Sal hired a hit man."

"Our *doorman* Sal? Are you crazy, Matthew? Why would Sal do that? Malcolm liked Sal. He gave him free chill pills. I'm sure the cops will give him a good turn on the spit, but *you* have more of a motive to kill our parents than Sal has. Why are you so quick to shut us up?"

Matthew pushed his sunglasses to the top of his bird's nest of hair. He gave me the double-barreled blue-eyed all-American stare. Now the gloves were coming off.

*Yes,* I thought. *Everyone* should *defend themselves in the safety of the living room now, because sooner or later, we will have to do it for real.*

"Don't look at *me*, Tandoori," Matthew said. "Even if I am fast enough to circle the block before the smell catches up with my fart, I *still* wasn't here last night, and I *still* haven't even visited this insane asylum since Christmas."

Harry was running his fingers over the piano keys in a dramatic thrumming riff, either Chopin or Liszt—I wasn't sure which.

Then he stopped playing and said to Matthew, "Who even knows if that's true, Matty? You could have used the service elevator, and you could still have a key. No one would have known you were here. And, *Hugo*—your room is right at the foot of the stairs. You had easy access to the penthouse."

Hugo put down the weights and jackknifed to his feet.

"I'm just a *kid*! I couldn't kill my own parents. What am I supposed to do without them? Get a job? I'm four-foot-eight. I'm in the fifth grade."

Then he spun on his heels and pointed his huge index finger at me.

"Tandy's got motive, too. She's the one who got the last Big Chop."

# 12

*Are you ready for the story* of the last supper? My last dinner with Malcolm and Maud, the evening they died? I'm about to tell you the whole truth and nothing but. Far more than I told the cops. I'm really starting to trust you, reader.

The fact is, that night I got in trouble big-time, and I was punished. And it just so happens that punishment was Malcolm and Maud's specialty.

As I mentioned earlier, my father had prepared a private dinner for the UN's ambassador from the Kingdom of Bhutan. His name is Ugyen Panyor, and he believes himself to be directly descended from Ugyen Guru Rinpoche, who brought Buddhism to Bhutan thirteen centuries ago.

Father had prepared *ema datshi*, the national dish of Bhutan. He substituted feta cheese for the yak cheese in the recipe because yak cheese is very hard to come by, even in Manhattan. But the rest of the meal was authentic, including the excess of chilies combined with tomato and garlic, and the side dish of traditional red rice.

The ambassador was polite but not effusive in his praise, and I took offense. My father was a serious foodie. He cooked; he savored; he even named me Tandoori, after West Indian cooking that is prepared in a clay stove called a tandoor. We had a restaurant-grade tandoor oven in our own kitchen, which I'd leaned against as I watched my father prepare that night's meal.

So when the ambassador didn't make mention of the obvious perfection of my father's meal, I decided to bring up a topic that had been expressly forbidden by my parents before the ambassador arrived: the refugees living in UN-supervised camps in Nepal.

Insurgents had sprung up in these camps, and some believed that they were the intelligence behind the bombings that had pounded the country before the parliamentary elections.

The ambassador refused to answer my questions about the lack of progress to repatriate the refugees; he just said, with a cheeky smile, "And when did you get your degree in the foreign service, Miss Angel?"

It was nervy of him to take me on.

I said, "You don't behave like an ambassador, sir. You behave like a politician."

The look on my father's face said everything.

## 13

After the ambassador had been escorted to the elevator, with apologies, my parents marched me right into their study—a library with a high vaulted ceiling and bookshelves lining every wall. Two glass-topped desks stood in the middle of the room, facing each other. Samantha's amazing framed photos of the family decorated the mantel above the fireplace, the only other available surface.

My mother's desk held not one, not two, but *six* computer monitors, which she used to track every burp and giggle of domestic, European, and Asian markets so she could trade in nanoseconds.

My father's übercomputer had one enormous screen. It

operated at warp speed and had massive storage capacity so that he could mine the scientific world on every front, synthesize the data, and adapt it to his needs. But neither of them was sitting at their computer that night. Instead, they stood in front of them, arms crossed, staring me down as if they could crush me with their gaze.

When my father finally began yelling at me for disgracing him in front of an important guest, Harry started banging out Wagner's *Die Meistersinger von Nürnberg* on the Pegasus to drown him out.

Punishment in our house was called the "Big Chop," and it was always fitted to the crime and doled out immediately.

"You must name every landmark in Bhutan in Dzong-kha, the national language." My father furrowed his brow. "I don't care if it takes you the rest of the night. If you make a mistake, you'll have to start again, Tandy."

I said, "I want sixty seconds with the computer. That's only fair."

"Sixty seconds with the computer comes with a penalty."

"I'll take it," I said.

I hadn't read any Dzongkha since my freshman year, so I needed a refresher, and I wanted to see a map of Bhutan's cities, too. I flipped on the computer and scanned the

Google Earth view of Bhutan and the nearby countries of India and Nepal.

Then the computer was switched off.

Malcolm said, "You turned our dinner party upside down, Tandy. This chop is appropriate, fair, and equitable, and furthermore, for your penalty, you must execute this task while standing on your head."

If you're from a normal family, you probably think that part was a joke. But it wasn't a joke, and I knew it.

I had never won an argument with my father, and I never would. I put a cushion under my head and walked my feet up the bookcase. I began my recitation with the high spots—Thimphu, the capital; Mongar, a town in the east—and finished the cities before naming the monasteries.

My mother was online, tracking trades in Asia, and I whispered to her, "Mother, please. I've done enough."

"Buck up, Tandy," she said, "or we'll double the chop."

I was released after an hour.

I told my father that the meal had been delicious, and that I had enjoyed it when it came back up almost as much as I had enjoyed it going down.

He chuckled and kissed me good night.

Maud patted my cheek and told me I had to work on my pronunciation a little, but all in all, I'd done a good job.

I went to bed and thought about what I'd done, not because I was sorry for offending the ambassador, but because I'd let myself get out of control. I didn't like that. The few times I'd been out of control in my life things had gone terribly, terribly wrong.

I don't usually let myself think about those times.

If you stick with me long enough, though, maybe I'll remember enough about it—and about *him*—to share.

# 14

After our little family meeting, we decided it was best to try to get some sleep and keep talking in the morning. But it felt like only seconds after I drifted off that I was awakened by the sounds of loud pounding and crashing somewhere in the apartment.

I didn't have a shotgun, so I grabbed a lacrosse stick that was leaning against the wall and ran from my room toward the noise.

Was someone else being murdered?

I found ten-year-old Hugo in his room. He was still wearing his Giants sweatshirt, and he was using a baseball bat to break up his four-poster bed.

As I entered the room, he swung the bat for the last

time, splintering the headboard, then began working on the bed frame with karate kicks.

"*Hey*. Hey, *Hugo*," I said. "Enough. Stop. Please."

I dropped my lacrosse stick and wrapped my arms around my little brother. I dragged him away from the bed and more or less hurled him toward the cushy, life-size toy pony that Uncle Peter had given Hugo when he was born.

We collapsed together onto the pony, my arms wrapped tightly around him. He could easily pick me up and toss me into the closet, but I knew he actually wanted me to keep him still and safe.

"What is it, Hugo? Tell me what exactly has made you go bug-nuts."

Hugo heaved a long sigh that could have stirred the posters of Matty up on the wall. Then he put his head on my lap and started to talk.

"I didn't hear anything, Tandy. I *should* have. Something horrible happened in there, and I totally failed them! If I've ever done anything to deserve the Big Chop, this is it. I was supposed to protect them. Malcolm said that would always be my job."

"Hugo, it wasn't your fault."

I stroked my little brother's hair and told him about crimes that had happened without anyone knowing intruders were in the house. One of the stories was about a family that had lived in Florida in 2009.

"They were very kind parents," I told Hugo. "They had adopted a lot of children with disabilities, and had a total of sixteen kids."

Hugo listened attentively.

"Eight of those children were asleep in the house when three intruders broke in, and in just a few minutes shot the parents to death and escaped. They weren't caught. And no one knows why they committed that horrible crime."

I realized that I was talking to myself, suddenly aware of the fact that maybe someday some other big sister out there would be telling her little brother about the great unsolved Angel Family Murders.

I couldn't let that happen.

Soon, I noticed that Hugo's breathing had slowed. He wasn't in a state anymore.

"It was late, Hugo, and you were asleep. Whoever killed them was intent on being silent and invisible. If Malcolm and Maud had screamed, you would've been right there. All of us would have."

A few minutes later Hugo was asleep, half on me, half on the unloved stuffed pony. And he left me alone with a question:

*Why hadn't my parents screamed?*

# 15

*After everything that had happened,* it was hard to believe I'd be able to sleep. But I dozed off as soon as I crawled back into my bed, only to wake up sweating and feeling like I'd traveled very far—but also like I'd been tied to a bungee cord and yanked back to my bed, hard.

I'd had a dream, and like most of my dreams, it was a memory, complete in every detail.

My twin brother, Harry, and I had just turned three.

Maud was carrying Harry piggyback and Malcolm was carrying me. I had my fingers twisted in my father's hair and my legs were hooked around his chest. I was grabbing onto his shoulders and pulling up because I was so excited, kicking him in the ribs to make him go faster.

I could already recite Victorian poetry from memory, but right then I only had one thing to say: "Harry, Mommy, lookit meeee, lookit meeee."

The four of us were at the small boardwalk amusement park at Coney Island, where Malcolm and Maud had come as kids before they got married.

Maud looked beautiful in this memory, if that's indeed what it was. She was wearing a butter-yellow sundress and her dark hair was curling around her face and she was beaming at Malcolm and me as she said to my brother, "You're going to love this, my angel. This is going to be a wonderful experience. I wish that *I* were going on the roller-coaster for the first time."

Oompah music was coming from the merry-go-round, and bright-eyed, happy people swarmed all around us. Other kids were on their parents' shoulders or holding their hands or giggling and weaving through the crowd at high speed. And there was the pervasive and incredibly delicious first-time smells of burnt sugar and popcorn.

We joined the line for the Cyclone, and as we reached the front, the train of roller-coaster cars braked with a loud metallic squeal. A man in a striped shirt and suspenders pulled a lever and the lap bars came up, releasing the people who had been on the ride. They spilled giddily down the ramp past us.

Now, no three-year-old would ever be legally allowed to ride on a coaster like the Cyclone, but Malcolm and Maud thought their children were up to the task. The man looked at us and shook his head, pointing to the height requirement. My father pulled out his wallet and quickly remedied the situation; several hundred-dollar bills, at least, must have changed hands. The man's face broke into a smile, and he tore our tickets and remarked on what pretty children we were. Our parents placed us next to each other in one of the seats, and then took the seat behind ours.

The metal bar came down across our laps and locked with a loud *clank*—although there was still a considerable amount of space between our bodies and the bar. The train began to roll forward. "Here we gooooo," Malcolm sang from behind me. "Hang oooooooon."

The car rolled slowly at first, chug-chug-chugging as it went up the incline. For a moment we hung over the boardwalk. We could see the moving dots of color below, and the other rides, and even the beach and the horizon.

And then, with a breathtaking and shocking suddenness, it all dropped away. My stomach flipped over and my eyes watered and I gripped the lap bar with both hands.

It was the most incredible feeling.

I was *flying*.

As the car hurtled toward the boardwalk, Harry let out

a piercing scream that could be heard over the shrieks of our fellow passengers—and probably across the whole island. I looked at him and saw that his face was crumpled, completely transformed by terror.

I turned away.

I could see myself as if from above, leaning into the wind, looking into the next dip and rise, feeling one with the roller coaster, seeing everything. I didn't want it to stop.

But it *did* stop—because of Harry's wailing, blubbering, unceasing meltdown. The man in the striped shirt slowed and then stopped the roller coaster as it pulled into the station.

The bars went up.

Malcolm reached toward me to lift me out of the seat, but Maud picked me up instead and said to Malcolm, "You take *him*."

We left Coney Island in a hurry. I wrapped my legs around Maud's waist and pressed my face against her sunny yellow bust. Harry clutched Malcolm's hand and was being dragged along, sobbing the whole way.

My father said sternly, "Buck up, son."

I never heard our mother call Harry "my angel" again. And for a long time, he was referred to as "the boy we found on the boardwalk."

I was three, and three was all about *meeeee*. But do I regret that I hated my brother for being afraid?

Profoundly.

After the murders I was consumed by sadness for my brilliant and lovable twin, who had never been considered good enough, and would never be able to confront our parents as an adult.

I wanted to give in to my grief for Harry, and for my mother and father, too. But no tears would come.

*What's wrong with me? Why can't I cry?*

# 16

*The day after my parents were murdered* was a Saturday. For the first Saturday morning that I could remember, Malcolm wasn't in the kitchen whipping up something green and stinking to infuse our brains with oxygen and steep our bodies in trace minerals.

There were also no calisthenics, no foreign-language drills, no pop quizzes on geopolitics or the state of the global economy.

The very atmosphere had changed.

It was as if one of the elements of the planet had disappeared; not water, air, fire, or earth, but something else. Maybe it was the rule of law, as Malcolm would call it.

I opened my computer and did a search for *sudden*

*deaths* and *black tongues* and found terrible things that raised my eyebrows as high as they could go. I began a folder of questions with both answers and hypotheses and was still absorbed in my detective work when the police arrived for a surprise visit at 7:30 AM.

Again, I was the one who heard the buzzer and let them in.

We stood in the hallway, under a chandelier shaped like a sci-fi UFO, and the police began to grill me right there under its bright, blinking lights.

Detective Hayes looked as though he hadn't changed his clothes from the night before. Sergeant Caputo wore a short-sleeved shirt and black slacks that stopped short of his black sneakers. He looked down at me as though I were a bug mounted in a lab.

"You didn't tell me you had a guest for dinner last night. Why did you withhold information, Toodles?"

Some people might have been embarrassed at being caught in a lie of omission by a crude cop with a tattoo of a goat on his wrist, but it didn't bother me. My parents had repeatedly told me that I had a "phlegmatic" conscience—which basically means it doesn't work overtime—and that that was a good thing. Was either part of that true? I had no idea.

I fake-smiled and said, "Are you pretending you don't

know my name, Sergeant Caputo? Or is jabbing a suspect an interview technique of yours? I really want to know. I'm learning your craft, and I'm a fast learner."

"You cost us valuable time, Candy. If we had known, we would have interviewed Ambassador Panyor last night."

"I'm not supposed to speak to you without my attorney, but I'll give you this for free," I said. "The ambassador didn't kill my parents. My father prepared all of the food, and I helped him. The meal was served in big bowls, family-style. My brother Harry and I ate everything my parents ate, drank everything they drank. We're both perfectly fine, and apparently so is the ambassador. You can't arrest him, anyway. He has immunity."

"You should have told me, Tidbit. I'm moving you to the top of my list," Caputo said.

He answered his phone, then opened our front door for a couple of CSIs. The three of them went upstairs to what I still thought of as my parents' room.

We had truly been invaded by aliens. Rude and very nasty ones. And there was nothing we could do to stop them from infesting our home planet.

# 17

*Funny moment in the middle of a tragedy.*

Detective Ryan Hayes sat down on the Pork Chair and it let out a snuffle, a snort, and a ringing squeal.

He jumped up. "What the...?"

"Art," I told him with a smile. A real smile, this time.

"Does the sofa bark or anything? Let me know now."

"The sofa is mute," I said.

"Fine," Hayes said, but he eased himself down gingerly anyway. "Sit down," he told me. "Please." He looked through the Plexiglas top of the shark tank that served as a coffee table.

"These are real sharks?"

"Pygmy sharks. Hugo won them."

"He won them? Like, at a carnival?"

I paused and decided it would be too hard to explain "Grande Gongos" just then. So I said, "These are real pygmy sharks. At an average of nine inches long, they are the second-smallest sharks in the world. Their stomachs glow green because they're bioluminescent—they have special phosphorescent cells in their skin. It's possible that the green light attracts prey to them. The sharks can't see you because the tank is specially designed to block light—"

Hayes interrupted my monologue. "Your mother was a bit like a shark, wasn't she, Tandy? No disrespect, but that's what I've heard. She worked all the time, but still, she had some pretty unhappy customers lately. Very unsatisfied customers."

"She wasn't exactly Bernie Madoff. My mother was honest. Honest people can have enemies. My mother said whatever she believed to be the truth."

"There was a massive lawsuit pending against her for manipulating investor returns. A man named Royal Rampling is at the helm of it. Ever heard that name before?"

My stomach lurched, but I ignored it. " 'In volatile times, not every client is a satisfied client,' " I said, quoting my dead mother. "Still. Let's say she had a particularly disgruntled client who happened to be a homicidal maniac as well. How could this...Royal Rampling"—I forced the name out with some difficulty—"have gotten in, killed her and my father—"

"We're looking at every possibility," said Hayes, again cutting me off. "Let's talk about something else. I wanted to apologize for my partner, Tandy. Caputo is a hound. Did you know that hare hounds can pick up the scent of a rabbit on concrete?"

"I did, actually," I said truthfully.

"Then you know that if a rabbit runs across the road, an hour later a hare hound can still smell that the hare has been there. Cap Caputo's like that. If there's a trail, he'll find it."

"Thanks for sharing. When will we get the autopsy report?" I asked.

Caputo was coming down the stairs and overheard me.

"There's no 'we,' Tammy. We're the cops. You're a suspect. Prime suspect, in my opinion."

"You may call me Tandy. You may call me Ms. Angel. But please don't ever talk down to me again."

"Or what?"

"Don't bother testing me, Sergeant," I warned. "Angels always, *always* ace their tests."

"All the more reason you make an ideal suspect. As far as I can tell, Angel is a pretty ironic name for this family."

"We don't particularly relate to the spirits, if that's what you mean."

"You know what I mean. You guys don't exactly wear halos."

"Neither do the thirty-four other Angels in the Manhattan white pages. Halos are *so* last season, anyway."

My attempt to sound like a normal teenager went over well. He smirked.

"Cute, kid. We're leaving now, but don't skip town. We'll be seeing all of you Angels again very soon. Especially you, Miss Indian Cooking Stove. Especially you."

# 18

*The police and CSI techs finally pulled down* the crime-scene tape at the top of the stairs and left our home, taking with them my parents' computer hard drives and notebooks, as well as cardboard file boxes filled with objects from my parents' bedroom.

A wave of inexplicable anger washed over me, which I immediately quelled. If only I had someone I could commiserate with about this invasion of privacy, about the way everyone was treating us like murderers instead of grieving children.

But I had no friends to call. I hadn't even thought about what it would be like to go back to school after everything that had happened, and I didn't trust anyone there, anyway. Since the murders, Harry and Hugo had been spending most of their time in their rooms. I was a loner, like they were, but I had never before felt loneliness quite like this.

I went to the semicircular bay window behind the piano and looked down onto Seventy-second Street to watch the police load up their vans with my parents' belongings. It was unlikely I would ever see these things again; I was certain they were doomed to languish in storage in some dark police facility.

A herd of reporters stampeded toward Hayes and Caputo, and then followed the cop cars and crime-scene vans on foot, shouting for attention as the police vehicles took off toward the precinct on West Eighty-second.

The band of reporters reassembled at the front gate, and I watched the attractive newscasters flipping their hair and fastening microphones to their collars, using the backdrop of the Dakota for their on-air reports.

I tried to imagine what Maud would have thought of all this, if she'd ever imagined her death at all. Surely she would have chosen something dignified at the age of ninety or so—maybe a quick cerebral hemorrhage after a full day of work. She wouldn't have wanted the *Post*, the *Daily News*, Fox News, and *Entertainment Tonight* fluttering around the building, picking at the details of her life. As much as she revered success, she detested the mass forms of communication that reported on the successful. Call it yet another contradiction that my parents embodied.

I went across the hall to our home theater, with its plush velvet seats lined up in front of a gargantuan screen that doubled as a television when we weren't watching movies (strictly educational films, of course). I clicked to a news station, and a reporter that I had actually just seen from the window was now looking out at me from the TV screen, saying:

"With his brother, Peter, Malcolm Angel owned Angel Pharma, a multinational drug company. Maud Angel was founder and CEO of a successful hedge fund, Leading Hedge, which has come under SEC scrutiny in the last few weeks.

"Still, the Angels died at the pinnacle of success. Their motto was 'yes we can,' long before Barack Obama campaigned with that slogan.

"The Angels leave four children ranging in age from ten to twenty-four. The oldest is the celebrated athlete Matthew Angel, who plays for the New York Giants. All four children are known to be high achievers—or, as some say, overachievers.

"But that figures into the Angel family reputation.

Malcolm and Maud Angel were referred to in their social circle as 'Tiger Mom and Tiger Dad.' And now the tigers are dead.

"The police have no comment, but if you're just joining us, *Inside News* has learned that the Angels' deaths have been termed 'suspicious.' We'll be bringing you further news on this story as it unfolds. Stay tuned to this station...."

No. I'd had way too much of the news already.

I turned off the TV and wandered out of the theater. The apartment was still cloaked in an eerie silence. Matthew and Hugo were in Hugo's room. Samantha's door was closed. And my twin typically sleeps late on Saturdays. That day, I thought, Harry might not get out of bed at all.

If I closed my eyes, I could almost pretend it was a normal weekend at the Angel house, with Malcolm and Maud off at work, putting in overtime. And I wondered: What would a *normal* family be doing less than twenty-four hours after discovering their parents had been murdered?

I suppose they'd be *together*, for one. There would still be a lot of tears, runny noses, wailing, and grinding of teeth. Lots of visitors coming over making sure everyone was okay, bringing food and things to make sure the grieving family members didn't have to worry about feeding themselves. Does that sound about right?

I wouldn't know. All I know is that we will never be normal. Because I wasn't thinking about any of that. Here's what I was thinking:

It was a perfect time to search the house—especially my parents' room. The scene of the crime.

# 19

*I have to admit* that by that point I had already become obsessed with solving my parents' murders. I should also confess that I'm a bit obsessive-compulsive anyway.

I took a self-guided tour of the downstairs rooms just to make sure that no stone had been left unturned, that no obvious forced entry had been missed. I thoroughly checked the family rooms: living room, hallways, library, and kitchen. I double-checked the laundry room and the back door and the elevator. I saw no nicks or breaks in the door frames, no scratches on the locks. I saw nothing out of place. Disappointing.

Everywhere I looked, I saw Angel family perfection.

I took to the stairs and noticed right away that I was finding it a little difficult to breathe. This was my parents' suffocating world, after all. But I was having an uncharacteristically emotional reaction to it.

Halfway up, I passed Mercurio, the larger-than-life sculpture of a merman hanging from his tail by a chain and a hook screwed into the ceiling. "Blood" was dripping down his chest, and there was a look of pure anguish on his face. Fitting.

Mercurio was another of Hugo's Grande Gongo "prizes," and another parental indulgence with a message: *Life is serious. You win or you lose, and winning is a lot better.*

My father had told us about the actual, real-life *Grande Gongo*, a cutting-edge container ship docked in Korea and flying the Italian flag. He'd said that the *Grande Gongo* was an "an intrepid craft on a mission—with no boundaries." And that was how he thought of his children.

Certificates of excellence had been hung on the stairwell wall, alongside mottos that my father had found important enough to frame. The one he never let us forget was written by a poet and priest who had died almost four centuries ago:

ONE FATHER IS MORE THAN A HUNDRED SCHOOLMASTERS. —GEORGE HERBERT

There was another framed item that I rarely passed without stopping to read it again. It was an envelope and letter from Hilda Angel—my father's mother—who died just before Malcolm and Maud were married.

Apparently, Gram Hilda had not approved of the marriage.

She had scrawled on the back of the envelope, *"Do not open until my will has been read."*

After the reading of her will, the letter was opened. It was in my grandmother's handwriting, and it was signed and notarized. Even the notary's signature had been notarized. It read:

*"I am leaving Malcolm and Maud $100, because I feel that is all that they deserve."*

Rather than feeling insulted, my parents had used Hilda's disapproval to fuel their financial aspirations. They had made millions and millions since Gram Hilda had disinherited them. Her letter was a Big Chop that was also a stupendous motivator.

I climbed to the top of the staircase, put my hand on the newel, and stepped into the second-floor hallway. My parents' killer had stood where I was standing now.

I shivered.

What had he been thinking as he primed himself for the kill?

# 20

*I walked down the long hallway* leading to my parents' suite, intending to pass through their bedroom doorway as I'd done so many times before. But when I got to the threshold, I found that I couldn't force myself to cross it. It was as if a thick glass wall had formed in the doorway and I couldn't get past it.

I stared through the imaginary glass and saw that their room had been officially trashed since I'd last been in there.

After the crime-scene techs had taken photos and fingerprints, they'd torn the room apart. Every single drawer had been emptied, clothes had been shoved aside in the closets, and carpets had been rolled up. The Aronstein flag painting was down and leaning against the wall, and my parents' four-poster bed had been stripped bare.

I had to face reality: The crime scene had been destroyed by the police, and there could be no useful evidence whatsoever still inside.

As I stared into the room, I flashed back to seeing Malcolm and Maud dead on their bed, that split-second glimpse of them locked and frozen in their death struggles. Like Robert and Mercurio, they had looked lifelike, but not alive.

The horror of it caught up with me again. I may live a very sheltered life, but that doesn't mean I haven't experienced a few unspeakable things. I've just managed to block them out.

But not this one. Not yet. It was too fresh.

I was struck by a wave of nausea and had to immediately cover my face with my hands and concentrate on my breathing. My eardrums pounded as blood pulsed through my brain, calling to mind that roller-coaster ride with Harry so many years before.

When I took my hands away and looked again at the room, I forced myself to concentrate as hard as I ever have in my life. I looked at each object and tried to compare it to my earlier flash inventory of my parents' possessions.

But here's the thing: I couldn't possibly know what the police had taken—or what might have been taken by an intruder the night of the murders.

I visualized my parents during their last hours alive, both in bed, wearing their reading glasses, books in their laps. I put myself outside their door. They looked up as I came in.

*Anything wrong, Tandoori?*

*Father. Who killed you and Mother?*

In my mind's eye, their faces were simply frozen in a look that I couldn't read. A look I'd never seen on their faces before that night.

A minute or two later, I left the master bedroom suite in a daze and went back downstairs—where I ran directly into Uncle Peter. He was carrying a glass of red juice in his hand. Maybe it was the morbid effect of living in a crime scene, but I imagined him drinking blood.

Which wouldn't really surprise me, actually. The guy was a vampire of a different sort. Sucked the life out of people. Heeded only his own survival instinct. I hate him for reasons that run so deep my conscious mind hardly has access to them.

"Watch it, Tandy."

I was almost glad to see him, but not for long. He was headed toward "his" room, had his hand on the door as he said to me, "I'm going to be using this room as my office, so please keep in mind: *Noli intrare.* No admittance. It's a new rule."

"What did you do to Katherine's room?"

"Out. *Out. Noli perturbare.* Do not disturb!"

And then my uncle Peter closed the door in my face. Can you see why I dislike him so immensely?

That's why it disturbed me so much to see him in Katherine's room. She and I had been extremely close, and I had spent many weekend mornings in my big sister's bed, with its pink crown of a headboard, gazing at the Marilyn Minter painting of lips and pearls on the opposite wall. I could tell her anything, and I learned more from her about the world outside our apartment than I ever did from my rigorous lessons with Malcolm and Maud.

I was particularly interested in her many stories about dating—secretly, of course. I asked a lot of questions, made a lot of mental notes. I even wrote a few things down. And Katherine was very free with her information. I think she felt bad for me and my lack of experience with what she called "the real world."

My sister was brilliant and charming and a beauty, just like my mother had been. To the rest of the world, Katherine appeared smart, curious, calm, together. But she was very different on the inside. She was able to feel real passion about things, about people. I really looked up to her. Everyone loved her.

Then she won the Grande Gongo—and it turned out to be the biggest chop of all.

It ended with Katherine's death.

# 21

When I walked in on Harry in his bedroom, I saw that tears streaked the sides of his face. He was awake, lying spread-eagle in his big platform bed, looking up at the trompe l'oeil painting of a domed and gilded ceiling that was open at the center to a pink sky. Angels peered over the rim and looked down on him. Seven Angels, to be exact—one for each member of our family. He'd painted them himself. How strange that Malcolm and Maud were staring down at him right now....

I sat on the side of the bed. "I brought you some lunch, okay?"

"I can't eat."

"It's very nice, Harry. I tasted it. No poison, I promise. Chicken with orzo and a touch of cilantro. Malcolm made it. I just found it in the fridge."

"Maybe we should freeze it. A keepsake. A memory."

"You know he wasn't sentimental like that. He would want you to eat it now."

Harry sat up and rubbed at his eyes with his palms. Then he leaned back against the bed and ate the soup. Some of it, anyway.

"Come on, bro. You have to eat. Buck up."

That was what our parents used to say. I wished I hadn't said it.

"I'll tell you what's killing me, Tandy."

"I'm listening."

"They never loved me."

"Come *on*. They were different, that's all—"

"One day I was going to prove myself to them. I never had the chance to do it before they died. They died thinking I was useless."

"They loved you," I said, hoping that Harry could find a shred of conviction in my voice. "They withheld praise. From all of us. You know that. It stunk, but it's how they raised us."

"Painting is for sissies. Piano is for wimps. Singing is for girly-men. I'm quoting them now."

"Did you actually believe them when they said that, Harry? They bought art and went to the opera. They let you paint and sing and play."

Harry paused, pondering yet another of Malcolm and Maud's puzzling contradictions. He finally shook his head.

"Remember when I played Carnegie Hall?"

"The first time? When you were ten and the youngest piano soloist at Carnegie Hall ever? You were amazing. I'll never forget that day, Harry. The audience rose to their feet, and must have applauded for at least five minutes. They totally adored you, and it was an audience that knew what they were listening to."

"Malcolm came late. Maud left early."

"But they had a party for you, remember?"

"I was ten. The guests were *their* age. Don't make excuses for them. I have to come to grips with this now and forever."

I took the soup bowl out of his hands and put it on the floor, then got into bed beside him. He rolled toward me and cried on my shoulder. It really hurt to hear Harry cry.

But I had to ask him. I had to. He was very creative, and I was pretty sure he could come up with a way to do the impossible and never get caught.

"Did you kill them, Harry?"

He drew back and looked at me, his eyes switching back and forth across my face.

"No," he finally said. "I didn't kill them, Tandy. Did *you*?"

It's one thing to ask someone if they're guilty. It's another to be asked. I was nonplussed.

"Because, Tandy," Harry went on, "I know what they took from you. I know we don't talk about it—about *him*. About the incident. But I'll never forget. How much it hurt. Both of us."

I just stared at him.

"Have you forgotten, Tandy?" he asked. "Have you?"

# CONFESSION

*My brother.* Sweet, gentle, weepy Harry. I swear he wouldn't knowingly do anything to hurt anybody. The real Harry wouldn't hurt a fly. Not even a hideous cockroach. When he was a little boy, he actually caught bugs in his hand and set them free on the fire escape—when Maud wasn't looking.

So how do I explain the *one* time in his life Harry hurt someone? The day when my twin betrayed the person who loves him the most? Sometimes I'm so glad I've been given the gift of control over my emotions, because I just can't even *imagine* how much it would have hurt me otherwise.

Harry never came to the hospital after my…incident. The most traumatic experience of my life. Malcolm and Maud wouldn't really say why.

"He's busy practicing" was Maud's weak explanation.

"He's never been good around blood or needles, you know that," Malcolm said, with a touch of disdain.

Hugo was the one who told me the truth—as usual. He was too young to lie about something like that. "Harry didn't come because he said you deserved it," he reported innocently. "Why, Tandy? Why did you deserve it?"

I looked away and didn't answer.

**22**

*And that's just what I did* this *time*, too, as Harry's earlier question echoed in the room: *Have you forgotten, Tandy? Have you?*

I looked away and didn't answer.

I lay next to Harry in his bed, watching the changing light reflect on the painted angels peering down from the ceiling. Harry had been inspired by Michelangelo's timeless masterpieces in the Sistine Chapel, and had invented his own special effect so that the angels' wings seemed to shimmer in every color against a lightning-struck pink and gold sky.

My mother found Harry's work sentimental. Maybe it was, but like his music, I found his paintings evocative, endearing, and curious. I didn't really connect to them in the way I think Harry hoped I might, but that was just a genetic issue. He and I had talked about how odd it was that we were called "twins" when we were really nothing more than siblings who happened to grow in the womb together at the same time. Fraternal twins come from two totally separate eggs, and the differences between us were obvious: I got all the scientific genes, and Harry got all the artistic genes.

Which made me wonder: Was Maud or Malcolm really an artist at heart? Were the Angel children their sculptures, their canvases, their creations to be put on display for all the world to see and admire?

Almost any other parents would have been proud of Harry. It was a mystery to both of us why his painting wasn't valued in this family. Maybe because it represented something missing from our lives. Or at least *my* life. Magic...soul...light?

Or love? Yes, maybe that was it. The experience of true, passionate love that had been snatched away from me just when it had been in my grasp—

*Nil satis nisi optimum*, interrupted my father's voice, booming inside my head. Crushing the thought as if it were vermin.

*Nothing but the best is good enough.*

He meant *no one* but the best is good enough.

*It doesn't matter anymore*, I reminded myself. *Only one thing matters now.*

"I'm going to find out who killed them," I said to my sleepy twin.

Harry laughed. "I was wondering when you'd decide you were the most qualified person to solve the crime. And that you could do it without a forensics lab."

"There were detectives before there were crime labs, you know."

"Fair point."

"Furthermore, I believe that Maud and Malcolm were poisoned."

"In your opinion."

"In my opinion," I said. "Based on my research."

Harry sighed and looked at me with his big, searching eyes. "You know, Tandy," he began. Then he stopped.

"What?"

"Even though you were the last one to get the Big Chop, I don't think you could have killed Malcolm and Maud. And I don't think you have to prove it *wasn't* you by solving the murder."

Did no one in this family understand me? I wasn't trying to prove my innocence. I was trying to bring whoever committed this crime to justice, *even if it turned out to be me.*

"The chop wasn't so bad," I said. "You just concentrate on the good times, like your Grande Gongos, and get through it."

I immediately regretted my words.

Harry had never been awarded the Grande Gongo. The rest of us had won it at least once—even Hugo, who was six years younger than Harry and I. He'd won it three times already. Hugo had also gotten one of the biggest chops in the history of the family, but that was another story.

As I was thinking about Hugo, he came into Harry's room and did a flying leap onto the bed, almost bouncing us out of it.

"You've got to get dressed, Harrison Weepyface."

Harry groaned and turned over, pulling his pillow over his head.

"He's got to get dressed," Hugo said to me. "He's going to be late."

I went to the closet and took Harry's tuxedo out of the dry cleaner's plastic. Then I half coaxed, half badgered him out of his bed and into the shower.

I left Harry in Hugo's care and called Samantha and Matthew on the intercom. Then I called Virgil, our driver and sometime bodyguard. He was fifty, and he was huge. Almost as big as Matthew. He wore a diamond in his ear.

He was a poet who wrote raps in his spare time. Virgil was also very kind to all of us kids.

"I'm very sorry about the terrible news, Tandy. I'm very, very sorry," he said when he saw me. He was a big bear of a man who didn't think twice about offering me a hug in the face of this tragedy. I accepted it awkwardly. Not because I didn't appreciate Virgil's gesture, but because hugs were a rather strange and rare phenomenon in our house.

"I'll bring the car around in about five minutes," he said.

Only moments later, I was wearing a black dress and heels, and Harry had been transformed from a waif in baggy clothes to the smartly dressed boy prodigy that we knew him to be.

My three brothers and Samantha rode down in the elevator with me. I held Harry's hand. He could have canceled, but even he knew that he would feel better once he poured himself into his work and was applauded for it.

It was a big day for Harry. He was playing a piano concerto at Lincoln Center.

# 23

*Avery Fisher Hall was packed* with music aficionados—more than *two thousand* of them. Harry was one of Mischa Dubrowsky's advanced students and was playing two pieces that day. He was the headliner, performing after six other gifted young pianists.

The hall is nothing like what you'd expect from seeing concert halls in the movies. There's no red velvet or chandeliers; instead, it's a magnificently simple place, the walls and ceiling paneled in light wood, to showcase the performance and the performer.

My brother Harry, my twin. Even after seeing him play in such magnificent spaces so many times, I still got excited for his moments in the spotlight.

There was an excited whisper in the hall as Maestro Dubrowsky came onto the stage in his tux, with his long mane and mutton chops. I got chills as he introduced my brother and said that he would be playing Bach's "Partita no. 1 in B-flat."

Harry strode confidently out from the wings, looking so handsome I could hardly believe he was the same boy who'd been staring up at his ceiling, wracked with grief, only an hour before.

Harry took the bench at the Steinway grand and paused for a moment with his fingers on the keys. Then he started to play. The audience was silent. In awe. Transported. I don't know very much about music—I'm the only one in the family who can't sing or play an instrument—but even I knew that what I was listening to was sheer magnificence.

Harry had told me all about Bach. He'd explained that Bach's music has a measured grace, an inherent tranquility and lightness, and that it is precise, almost mathematical. "That's why you'd like Bach, Tandy," he'd said. "He's not bombastic like Brahms, or romantic like Chopin." At which point I probably kicked him in the shins. But he was right.

Bach was a kind of expression I could connect with.

Harry had told me that Bach should be played very softly, and very loudly, to exaggerate the phrasing, because the pieces themselves are so ordered that the emotion needs to come through in the playing.

I listened for these elements as Harry lost himself in the music. I lost myself, too, as the music captured me in the way that only great music can.

I thought I felt a catch in my throat, and I caught myself.

And I thought of Harry as a little boy of three, sitting at the huge piano in the bay window of the living room, his legs too short to reach the pedals and his hands too short to span a chord. And still, he practiced. Four or five hours a day, every single day, without fail.

I was brought back to the moment by the man sitting to my left, who seemed overcome by Harry's rendition of the piece. His eyes were wet and he tapped his fingers on his knees and moved his head in time to the music.

I looked back to the stage. I knew that the climax of the piece came on with the gigue, the lively, fast-paced finale, and Harry was rendering it perfectly and faithfully, but with the brilliant accenting that the critics had always acclaimed as uniquely his.

As the last notes of Harry's performance rang through the auditorium, the man to my left turned to me and exclaimed, "That Harrison Angel is a true genius! Perhaps our greatest pianist. And he's only a young boy!"

I said, "I know. I know."

I stood up to applaud, along with two thousand other admirers. Harry dipped his head in a bow, and then again when the audience continued clapping.

It's possible that my twin was the brightest of all the Angel kids. The one of us with the most potential. Why couldn't my parents see this? What was wrong with them?

And was that why they had been murdered?

## 24

*We were feeling exhilarated* after Harry's magnificent performance, and we were also starving.

The five of us rode up in the north elevator, taking turns listing the goods stored in our pantry by food group. Whoever named the fewest foods would have to cook. This is the way we Angels play.

"Get ready to make dinner, Sam," I told her. She didn't know the pantry like we did. Most kids from a family like ours wouldn't know the first thing about the kitchen, either, since it was usually the territory of the cook or housekeeper, but Malcolm had us all regularly cooking from the age of seven.

"You'll be sorry if I do," she said. "You know me. I'm the microwave queen."

"Never too late to learn to be great," Hugo said, and we all laughed. Another quote from our father.

We exited the elevator on the top floor and found the front door to our apartment wide open.

Samantha got out her phone and said, "I'm calling nine-one-one."

Matthew's chest, arms, and forehead seemed to expand, and the muscles in his neck thickened. "Stay here, all of you. I'm going to see who's in there." His bluer-than-blue eyes blazed like guide lights on an airfield at night.

He was heading through the open doorway when Sergeant Capricorn Caputo stepped into view. He put out his hands to stop Matthew from bulling into the apartment.

"You don't have to call the police, Ms. Peck. We're already here. We still have a search warrant, and we're executing it."

The police had entered our house when we weren't there. It was another scandal in a day of many.

Uncle Peter was sitting on the red couch, his cell phone in hand. When he saw me, he covered the mouthpiece and said to me, "They're authorized, Tandy." Then he went back to his phone call.

The uniformed cops inside the apartment ignored us, coming and going through the kitchen and using the service elevator, taking cartons of foodstuffs with them.

"What the hell are you people doing here?" Matthew shouted.

I ignored Matty's outburst. "Have you gotten back the medical examiner's report?" I asked Caputo as calmly as possible. "There's only one conceivable option: My parents were poisoned."

"There's a backlog of bodies at the morgue, Tookie. So save us some time, why don't you. What poison did you use?"

"I did some research and found that a black tongue is caused by arsenic and by heparin," I said. "That help you any?"

"Arsenic poisoning is very painful," Caputo said. "It was probably a very bad death. Do you understand me? The killer showed no mercy."

*No mercy.* The words echoed in my mind. And that's when a very strange thing happened.

I suddenly felt as though my head had filled with helium. Caputo went in and out of focus. I felt Matthew's hand at my back. And then I heard people calling my name.

I opened my eyes and I realized that I was flat on my back on the floor. I recognized the pattern on the carpet. It was definitely our carpet. I had *fainted*.

I had passed right out in front of the cops.

I had totally disgraced myself.

*Mother, Mother, I'm so sorry.*

*Please forgive me.*

# 25

Samantha was only an inch or so from my face. "Tandy, say something, *please*." She offered me a glass of water, but I shook my head.

"I'm...okay. I don't know what...It's nothing. I'm fine."

Caputo's smirking features loomed in my vision. He squatted down next to me and said, "Let me tell you something, Tootsie. This could be your best chance to get ahead of what you did by confessing."

"Do you have any other suspects?" I asked him, getting to my feet. "Or is it the Angel kids and no one else?"

"We like the direction the case is going. Based on my conversations with your uncle, I think your parents might have had an inkling about which of you was out to get them," said Caputo. "Not to mention that I hear from multiple sources that you're the smartest kid in the family. I think that *you* thought you could get away with it. Why? Did you want their money?"

If I were a different person, I would have pointed out how absurd that last part was. What did I need money for? I was practically born in a bank vault. From day one, I had access to as much money as I could ever want.

Just not as much access to light, air, and freedom.

I ignored the impulse to berate him, because more than anything, I wanted to hear what Caputo knew. As Harry had pointed out, I didn't have a crime lab at my disposal. Right now, Caputo was my best source of information. I would have to draw him out. This was *my* Q&A, not his.

I said, "Sergeant, what prompted this new search? You've already torn the penthouse apart."

"We found a bottle in the trash room, Sassy. Inside that bottle was a trace of poison that matches the poison we found in a water glass we took from your parents' bedroom."

The cops had forensic evidence; that was news. I knew the glasses he was referring to—the handblown Venetian-glass tumblers Malcolm and Maud had kept beside their bed.

"So are you saying that someone made them drink the poison, then threw the bottle in the trash? That's absurd."

"Absurd? I call it *stupid*, but you've got a better education than I do."

"You know what I mean," I said. "Why would someone leave a bottle with poison in it where the police could find it?"

"Criminals make mistakes all the time," Caputo said.

Samantha interrupted us. "Come on, Tandy." She took my arm and led me to a chair. Then she said to the sergeant, "If you're not arresting anyone, we'd like you to leave."

"Yeah," said Hugo. " 'We're done here.' Isn't that what they say on all the police shows?"

"We're done for now. But I'm telling you again," Caputo warned, "don't go anywhere."

"If that's what we're being ordered to do, then I guess you'll be giving us a note excusing us from school."

"The noose is tightening," Caputo said. "You feel a little short of air, Snazzy?"

The funny thing was, I still did.

# 26

*Okay, so how am I doing so far?* I'm trying so hard to tell the story as objectively as I can, but it's not easy. I know I keep getting a little bit off track and letting my emotions about this—about *them*—get in the way, but I'll try to stick to the facts. That's what Malcolm and Maud would want me to do.

I got up early the next morning, ready to begin my own investigation in earnest. I was going to beat Caputo at this. He was barking up the wrong tree—no Angel kid would try to kill Malcolm and Maud. No way.

I stopped in the living room and fed canned clams to Hugo's sharks, then had a breakfast of cold leftover spaghetti and root beer. After I ate, I took the back stairs down one flight to Mrs. Hauser's apartment, which is right under ours.

Dakota residents are a very private clan. We don't want anyone to know our business, and if you don't believe me, google *the Dakota* and read about us for yourself. We don't talk to strangers, and we're certainly not keen on talking to the police. But as a resident, I have special access to my neighbors.

I'm also capable of behaving sweetly when I need to.

Mrs. Hauser's doorbell was made from a gold Sovereign dating back to the reign of King Edward IV. I pressed it. Chimes rang, and then I heard faint and irregular footsteps tapping on a parquet floor, coming toward the door.

When the door opened, our little bent-over downstairs neighbor, Sigrid Hauser, was standing there in a gauzy lavender-hued peignoir.

Her face crumpled when she saw me.

"Tandy, dear Tandy. Come in, come in."

Even though I really don't like to be touched, I let Mrs. Hauser hug me. It was surprisingly calming. Then I followed behind her at a very creaky pace until we were in her parlor, the décor of which was even older and mustier than she was.

"Mrs. Hauser, if you don't mind," I said, sinking into the ancient brown-velvet sofa. A stuffed springbok with horns and glassy amber eyes stared at me from over the fireplace, and for a moment I forgot what I was going to say.

"Anything you need, Tandy, just ask. Do you have enough money to get by?"

"That's all taken care of, Mrs. Hauser. Thank you. I just wanted to ask you if you know why or how someone could have gotten into our apartment? The doors were all locked that night."

Mrs. Hauser is a widow, and although she seems to be a frail old lady, I know she's shrewd; she's a very smart—though old and crumbly—cookie.

"Those policemen asked me the same thing, Tandy, and I cannot imagine how anyone could have entered your apartment without a key. I'm stumped on that one."

I nodded. "So am I, Mrs. Hauser."

"But there was something that I didn't tell the police, because it is none of their business," Mrs. Hauser said. She paused, slightly uncomfortable. "Can I get you anything? Would you like some herbal tea?"

"What didn't you tell the police?" I pressed, even though I completely understood why she wouldn't want to tell them something. I thought of my occasional impulse to leave out facts, like the ambassador's visit.

"Your momma and poppa were having an argument," Mrs. Hauser told me. "I was in the elevator with them, and they were very tight-lipped because I was there. But when I got out on this floor, they started shouting, and I could hear them right through the doors."

This was interesting. "What was the fight about?"

"Your father was saying that he was rearranging the finances and that was that. Your mother called him a name."

"Is that a quote, Mrs. Hauser? Exactly what he said?"

"Precisely."

"And Maud called him a name?"

"I'm afraid she did."

"What was the name she called him?"

"Oh, Tandy. I don't want you to think ill of your parents. I probably should have kept my foolish mouth shut."

"I've never thought of you as foolish," I said. "You're one of the wisest people I know."

Mrs. Hauser is neither the smartest nor the most foolish person I know, but I would have told her she was smarter than Marie Curie if it meant she would tell me what my mother had said.

"I'm sure they apologized to each other before they died. They must have."

"I'm sure they did, Mrs. Hauser," I said. "They were very forgiving. Please just tell me what my mother said."

"Maud called Malcolm a *boob*, Tandy. That's exactly what she said."

# 27

"No, *please, Mrs. Hauser.* I can find my way out. This has been really helpful. Thank you."

I left Mrs. Hauser sitting in her silky purple cloud under the springbok so that she didn't have to battle her arthritis just to walk me to the door.

But her words accompanied me, and although I didn't doubt her, it was hard to picture my parents fighting in public. And even harder to imagine my mother calling Malcolm a *boob.*

If I were a normal girl, it might even have made me laugh just a little. It sounded so…*immature.* Malcolm was one of the smartest men in the western hemisphere. Even when he was wrong, every decision he made was well thought out and reasoned. My mother must have been truly furious. So the word *boob* was nothing more than a clue that didn't lead anywhere.

Next I spent some time turning over the phrase *rearranging the finances.*

Had my parents' fight centered on Royal Rampling, the man who was suing my mother for fifty million dollars? His name gave me serious twists in my stomach. I can't even begin to explain why. But the fact is, if my father thought that we might lose the lawsuit, "rearranging the finances" could have been a way to protect the family from a crushing financial blow.

Then I had another thought.

Did this have something to do with Uncle Peter and the company he and my father owned? I thought about what Caputo had asked Samantha: *Who stands to benefit from the deaths of these people?*

Samantha didn't know, and even if she did, she would die before she would discuss my parents' private business. But honestly, it was obvious that my uncle Peter had the most to gain. With my father's death, he would become the sole head and major stockholder of Angel Pharma. That would *not* be small change.

As far as I knew, Uncle Peter didn't have a key to our apartment. And if he had come to the apartment late that night, Maud would have thrown him out of her room, not knocked back a shot of poison.

I closed Mrs. Hauser's door and pushed the elevator call button. The doors opened immediately, and inside the elevator was another of our neighbors.

His name is Morris Sampson, and I hate him.

I don't use the word *hate* lightly. In fact, I can't think of another person I hate as much as Morris Sampson.

If hate could kill, Morris Sampson would be *dead*.

# 28

*Despite the obvious excuse* I could have used to avoid Mr. Sampson—that I was traveling back up to my apartment instead of down to the lobby—I stepped into the elevator and said hello. I knew I couldn't miss an opportunity to interview another one of our neighbors, no matter how distasteful I found him.

Sampson looked good for a man of forty, and I would have expected nothing less than an impeccable presentation from a twenty-four-karat-gold narcissist who got paid sums of money for telling lies in the most pedestrian prose imaginable.

He said, "Hello, Tandy," and jabbed at the button for the ground floor.

JAMES PATTERSON

I hate Morris Sampson because he is a somewhat famous mystery writer who wrote a roman à clef, a novel that is obviously based on true events and real people. The villain in his book was a character called Maeve Engle, and, like my mother, she was a hedge-fund manager. The "fictitious" Maeve Engle was arrogant, cruel, greedy, and unethical, and she was murdered for it.

After Sampson's book came out Maud sued his publisher, and in order to settle the suit and quiet the bad publicity, the publisher had the books removed from the shelves and then put it out of print.

But the damage had been done.

People who had never questioned my mother's honesty suddenly did. It was probable, in fact, that the only reason Maud was being sued was because of the cloud Morris Sampson had hung over her head.

My mother became even more distant than she had been before—more removed from the world, and more removed from us.

Not long after the book scandal, I'd gone to Sampson's apartment and we'd exchanged quite a few angry words. It had been a nasty fight. I told Sampson that he was not only a very bad person, but a bad writer, too. That his books couldn't compare to the works of Ruth Rendell or

James Ellroy, and that he wasn't even fit to tie Elmore Leonard's shoes.

He knew I was right, and I knew that I'd hurt him.

But for this encounter I had to show him a different side of myself. I thought hard and put on a sad expression, the face people would expect to see on a girl whose parents had been killed just thirty-six hours before.

"Can you spare me a few minutes, Mr. Sampson?" I said as the elevator settled with a thump on the ground floor.

Sampson gave me a fleeting look, then stepped out of the elevator, holding open the doors as he said, "I don't have time for your games, Tandoori. Are you really sad that your parents are gone? Really?"

"That surprises you?"

"Surprised that you have feelings? Ha! Well, your parents were perfectly acceptable people, I suppose, and yet, I don't think the Residents' Committee will be honoring them with a plaque in the courtyard."

"Nice use of sarcasm, Mr. Sampson. A-plus."

"I dislike you, Tandy, but good luck," Sampson spat. "And give my best to your siblings—especially Harrison. He's the nice one."

Sampson turned away and let the doors go. Before they

closed, I found myself shouting, "You're a fleabite, Sampson! An *infected* fleabite!"

I heard him laugh; then I was alone in the elevator car.

I'd lost my temper. And that meant Morris Sampson had won.

Sampson was despicable, and he hated us, too, but hate alone didn't create poison in bedside water tumblers. If he had killed my parents, I couldn't imagine how he could have pulled it off.

If he had done it, it was the crime of the century. Morris Sampson wasn't smart enough for that. To be honest, he wasn't as smart as any of us Angels.

Not even close.

# 29

So *what do you think so far,* reader? Am I missing any clues? Am I doing a good enough job in my investigation? Would Malcolm and Maud be proud of my work?

That last question is an easy one. No. They wouldn't be proud until I had achieved my goal, and I was still so far from it.

Nathan Beale Crosby lives next door to us. In fact, his duplex apartment is an absolute mirror of ours. The big man with the red-framed glasses is a documentarian of note, making him one of the more famous residents of the Dakota. He has made a number of shocking and successful films, including *Meat Cage, Terror on the Street Where You Live,* and *Party Animal.* His work has won him an

Oscar, a bunch of Emmys, and some other awards that I don't pay much attention to. (I don't like most movies. I'm a reader. I read a lot. In my humble opinion, the prescribed story structure, the limited length, and the other restrictions inherent to film cause the truth to be treated as a handicap. Manipulating the audience is considered good form. But that's neither here nor there; my focus was on murder, not movies.)

Nathan Beale Crosby comes across as a very nice man, but he actually isn't. Unlike Morris Sampson, though, Nate pretends to be friendly.

A year ago he had a quiet dinner with my parents. He said he wanted to make a film about them, and he assured them that it was going to blow up the perception of wealthy entrepreneurs as predators and show the Angels as "American heroes."

Malcolm had said to Maud, "Sure, I believe Mr. Crosby. And Sarah Palin should believe Michael Moore if he tells her he wants to interview her for a puff piece on the Tea Party."

So, in other words, my parents declined the opportunity to be the subjects of a Nate Crosby film. Some time later, I found a film treatment on Crosby's website. A sketch, really. It was called "Filthy Rich."

It was about the Angels, to be sure, but I couldn't tell if

Crosby was going to savage us or if the title was a setup designed to seduce viewers before overturning their preconceptions.

At any rate, the film project never happened, at least not to my knowledge. Nate Crosby continued being friendly, and my parents liked him as much as they liked anyone at the Dakota.

But for the purposes of my investigation, it didn't matter if my parents liked him or not. I was a detective. And since some of Crosby's rooms abutted ours, he was an obvious person to interview. Had he heard anything the night "my folks"—as Detective Hayes called them—were killed? Did he have any theories about the murders?

I put my ear to his front door and heard faint sounds coming from inside. I pressed the doorbell, counted to thirty-five, and then pressed it again.

Finally I heard the metal clanking of the latch being turned, and then the door opened.

"My goodness, Tandy Angel! The spitting image of your mother, God rest her soul. We have so much to talk about. Please, come right in."

Nate Crosby's sandy hair was combed from back to front, and he wore a yellow cardigan and dark gray slacks.

"Tandy, I was just about to call you, but I didn't want to intrude. Please come in. I've been feeling awful about what happened, and wondering if I could help in any small way. Where are your brothers? Will you be taking some time off from school?"

I murmured that I hadn't really thought about it yet, but would discuss it with my siblings later. I thanked him for his kindness and followed him into the heart of the living room, a clean and monkish space that hardly looked lived in. A large flat-screen television was mounted over the fireplace; I looked up to see a network newscaster talking about my parents, a picture of Malcolm and Maud floating next to his head.

"I'm so sorry about that," Mr. Crosby said. He picked up the remote and switched off the set. I sat down across from him in a slatted wooden chair.

"What can I do to help you, Tandy? You and your brothers can count on me for anything."

I told him that my uncle Peter had moved in temporarily and that Matthew was taking care of Hugo, but that I had some questions.

"Did you notice anything unusual, Mr. Crosby? I thought that with your cinematic eye, you may have noticed something that no one else would have seen."

Crosby started to smile, then held it back in a way that made him look seriously constipated. "I've been thinking along the same lines, Tandy. After the police left, I scrutinized my memories for anything out of the ordinary, anything your parents may have said to me, or anything that struck me as remarkable."

"And did something come to you?"

"No, I'm afraid not." He gave me a kind but patronizing look. "What was remarkable was how much they loved all of you. They considered all of you so precious— and even more so after your sister died."

Listening to Nate Crosby's drivel was almost as bad as

enduring potshots from Morris Sampson. And frankly, both of them had a motive for killing my parents.

With the Angels dead, Morris Sampson could write another book about them—and probably not get sued. Unless *I* sued that nasty little man...

Which begged the question: Were the Angel children next on the killer's hit list?

Nate Crosby could make his documentary, and with us out of the way, he could tell our family's story any way he wanted.

My eyes must have glazed over as I considered these possibilities. I came back to myself at the sound of Nate Crosby saying my name.

"Tandy, when may I call on your family?"

"We'll see you at the funeral," I said, and without adding a thank-you or a good-bye, I got up and left Crosby's apartment.

There was a meeting scheduled in our apartment, and I was already late.

# 31

Our family's psychologist, the noted—and controversial—
Dr. Florence Keyes, was in the living room when I got
there. She was talking with Samantha, who had called for
the session.

Dr. Keyes looked up when I entered the room and said,
"Hi, Tandy, sweetie. Come sit down."

We'd known Dr. Keyes our entire lives, it seemed.
She'd been training all of us to "deal with" our emotions
since we were old enough to throw tantrums. We each
saw her once a month, on different days—I was every
second Tuesday—but never in a group setting like this. I
wondered if it would make things more difficult to do this
together.

Hugo had been doing pretty well with mastering his emotions, somehow channeling them all into his physical strength. Matthew stopped going to sessions the second he graduated from high school, which probably explained why he's now so prone to outbursts—say, for example, the Heisman incident. He didn't used to be that way.

And poor Harry...After eight years of intensive therapy, Dr. Keyes asked to start seeing him once a week. She just couldn't break through to him. Harry told me she never tired of coming up with new theories and methods for working with him. I'd observed the way she stared at him—almost like he was a great, raw diamond, just waiting for her to cut and polish to her liking. He was her greatest professional challenge.

I had a feeling Samantha was particularly concerned about how Harry was going to handle our parents' deaths. He was already like a ticking emo bomb. When was he going to explode?

As for me, well, I was Dr. Keyes's star patient. I was virtually a living, breathing manifestation of her doctoral thesis, "Binding the Soul: One Doctor's Quest to Eradicate Emotionality in the Interest of Moving Humanity into its Next Evolutionary Phase."

Once we were all assembled, Dr. Keyes settled carefully into the Pork Chair. She smiled at the freaked-out lot of us who faced her across the shark-tank coffee table.

"Before we start talking," she said, "let's remember that you're all going to be okay. You'll get through this. Your parents have provided for you. You are all smart, capable children who have been prepared for anything and everything—even this, the ultimate tragedy. You are strong. Stronger than most adults. There's nothing to fear. *Believe* in yourselves!"

There was a lot of shuffling and staring.

"Do you all believe in yourselves?"

"Yes, ma'am!" Hugo chirped. It was all a game to him.

"Perfect. Who else believes in himself? Matthew? I haven't seen you in so long, dear. How have you been?"

"Our parents were just *murdered*, for God's sake," Matthew said, leaning forward, clenching his fists. "I hated Malcolm and Maud. But no one had the right to do that to them. No one!"

Dr. Keyes said, "Matthew, I understand. You have every right to be angry. But let's remember the exercises we did together years ago, dear, to dissolve the anger, rid yourself of this poison. It's all mind over matter—"

"Murdering two people in their bed is *unconscionable*. I'm mad enough to kill someone *myself*. And I wouldn't be

133

"What? Do you have new information?" I asked eagerly. "About who might have done this?"

"No. It's about the funeral." Matthew swallowed. It was interesting to see him falter for a moment at that word. Then he quickly collected himself and resumed his big-brother-in-charge tone. "We have to figure out who's doing the eulogy."

We all stared at one another. That had been the furthest thing from our minds.

"Well, obviously not me," Harry piped up. "You know I'll self-destruct."

"Of course, Harry," I reassured him. "We wouldn't put you through that. You'll play a beautiful piece in their honor."

"Well, it's not going to be me, either," Matthew announced. "Sorry, I know you guys might think it's the role of the oldest, but I just had to put it out there that it's not an option, okay? I'm dealing with . . . some *stuff* right now."

I gave him a quizzical look. "Stuff?" Stuff, as in *guilt*?

"I'm sorry to hear it, bro," Harry said with a sarcastic look. "I thought we were all dealing with some *stuff* right now."

Matthew ignored him. "Hugo would be great," he continued. "Hugo, you're so upbeat and positive. Everyone loves kids. Especially when they get all poetic in a kidlike way..."

"About their dead parents," Harry finished. "Brilliant, Matty." Harry is so much better at sarcasm than I am.

"Are you nuts?" Hugo asked. "I'm ten. I'm officially *not responsible* for *anything.*"

"Of course not," I reassured Hugo. "We wouldn't put you through that. You'll be a pallbearer. The best, strongest pallbearer ever."

"Tandy's the obvious choice," Harry said with an encouraging nod at me. "You'd be in complete control. You'd say all the right things, and you wouldn't spill a tear."

That was a compliment, right? Yes, I reasoned. It was.

So why was I feeling a little...offended?

Matthew dug in. "No offense, Tan, but that's the problem. No emotion. Screw Dr. Keyes, man. Who wants a robot up there speaking at a funeral?"

# 34

*I left the living room* without saying anything to anyone. Harry called after me, but I just kept walking—yes, *robotically*—down the hallway to my room.

I entered the space that had been my safe place ever since I could remember and closed the door before someone saw me do something I would never live down.

I sat cross-legged on my bed and looked through the window at my grand view of Central Park. The fluffy treetops were like a green reflection of the clouds above, and there was a wide band of blue between the canopy and the sky.

I hardly understood what was going on as my throat tightened up and my gut began to heave. I started to break down. Before I knew it, I was shaking and croaking and gasping for air. And that quickly turned into sobbing, which wracked my body with convulsions that threw me facedown on the bed in a big wet mess.

I couldn't stop. I couldn't turn off the cascade of feelings that I didn't fully understand.

*I am not a robot.*

When I was finally able to take a few breaths without shuddering, I wiped my face with my sleeves and sat very still. I had no previous experience with all-out grief, but I had to admit the obvious:

I missed my parents, and I was scared. About what this would do to each of my siblings, and about what my siblings would do to one another. And about what would happen if one of them really was guilty. Would I protect him as fiercely, and without conscience, as my parents had protected me?

But there was more. I realized I'd lost something that until that moment I hadn't appreciated. My parents were supposed to live until they were so old that they *wanted* to die. I was supposed to learn from them, and fight them to the wall every time we disagreed, and eventually go into the world on my own.

Now I understood that an unspoken promise had been broken. As unreasonable as it may seem to you, friend, I was furious at them for abandoning me and Harry and Hugo and even Matthew, who hated them. I felt betrayed.

For one thing, I had never forgiven them for Katherine's death.

It was a hard kernel of anger that I could barely stand to examine.

And there was another thing I'd never forgiven them for.

# CONFESSION

*The kiss.* Destroyed. Forever. Malcolm and Maud ruined it.

It was my first kiss. It was once the most precious moment in my life, an experience I could relive and savor and examine from new angles, like a piece of fine art. Now it was like a worthless forgery. I couldn't see it in my mind's eye, couldn't feel it, couldn't even truly remember it.

I only believe it actually happened—almost as if in another life—because I wrote it down. And honestly, friend? I wonder sometimes if I just *made it up*, like a silly little fairy tale hastily scrawled by a pathetic, caged child.

When I stopped sobbing, I pulled my diary from its hiding place under my bed and found the page where it is written. The book fell open to the page immediately, since I've reread the words so many times:

> What I remember most is that the laws of physics no longer seemed to apply. Gravity was backward and the world was, I'm quite certain, moving in slow motion. His pull wasn't a pull; I was just falling upward, and he caught me. There really was no beginning or end to the kiss; it wasn't even really there—and because of that, it was tremendous. Our lips were just four sweet, shy people meeting, saying, "Hello, it's nice to meet you." But what passed between them was massive. Nuclear. And in an instant, every cobweb inside me was obliterated. My inner struggles, my uncertainty, my fear of tiger attack…gone. Just the feeling of being a newborn, a pure soul just waiting to be imprinted upon.

I slammed the book shut. Even after all this time, it reads as nonsense.

# 35

*A knock at my door* interrupted my thoughts.

I called out to whoever it was, "I'm not here. Go away, please."

But there was another, more insistent knock. "Tandy, may I come in?" Samantha asked.

I didn't want to see Samantha, or anyone else, but the knob turned and she came in anyway. She sat next to me on my bed.

"I miss them, too, Tandy. I'm sure your mother always wanted the best for you. But you know, she was complicated. A woman of many secrets."

"What do you mean?" I searched Samantha's face.

She seemed more shocked by what she'd said than I was. Whatever she had meant, she now choked it back.

"What secrets?" I asked.

"Oh, you know," Samantha said. "Her past. Her mother and father...weren't good to her. She never told you kids much about all that."

"You can tell me now, Samantha," I said. "She's dead." I gulped. It was harder to say that than I'd expected.

Samantha just shook her head. It was as if she still didn't believe it yet, still felt she couldn't ever tell Maud's business to anyone. "We have to accept them as they were, with all their faults." And then she was sniffling, too.

Samantha was the last person to see my parents alive, but I hadn't thought for a moment that she could have killed them. She had no motive to kill Malcolm and Maud, because she had absolutely nothing to gain. She no longer had a *job*. And soon, she wouldn't have a place to live, either.

I looked into her pink-rimmed eyes.

"Do you know who killed them?"

She shook her head.

I said, "I *do* accept them, Samantha, whoever they really were. I'm going to give the eulogy at their funeral. I wonder what I'm going to say."

# 36

My *mother had secrets;* Samantha obviously had secrets; and so did I. Now I think I'm ready to tell you a really big one.

Uncle Peter must have come back on the scene, because he and Matty were shouting at each other just outside my room. So I turned on some music and took out my pillbox.

The pillbox, which once belonged to Gram Hilda, is made of ebony and inlaid with mother-of-pearl. I opened the box and saw that I'd forgotten to take my pills the night before.

It was the first time I'd *ever* forgotten my medication. *Ever.*

I was horrified—probably because my parents would've been so angry with me. I could've even gotten a Big Chop for this. The same was true for my brothers, and for Katherine, when she was alive.

*You never miss your meds.*

I shook out the day's dose of candy-colored pills and held them in the palm of my hand: two green pills, one pink one, three white caplets, one multicolored round pill, two tiny black ones, and a yellow gelcap.

These were Malcolm's special super-vitamins, which he'd brought home from the factory for us ever since we were kids. I'd looked for them in the *Physicians' Desk Reference* and in the Angel Pharma catalog, but I'd never found matches for them. I had always suspected that our pills were Malcolm's off-label special blend.

"They're why you children never get sick," he'd say if we asked. And since we were the only kids we knew of who pretty much never got sick, there was no reason not to believe him.

But I hadn't taken my pills the night before—had missed just one dose—and then I had fainted, had an emotional breakdown, sobbed, and felt out of control. In short, I'd acted in a way that was just not like me.

I felt...like a lot of other teenage girls must feel.

Could this be...normal?

I wasn't sure what to make of it yet. But an idea was forming. It was not an entirely new idea, but it had never before seemed so powerful. And scary.

Why were the Angel kids so special, so different from other people and from one another?

Were my laser focus and concentration, Matthew's speed and agility, Hugo's strength, and Harry's artistic talent enhanced by this daily handful of pills? Had our father found some way to help us become more perfect, as good as we could possibly be, maybe even a little... supernatural?

If so, *what would happen if we stopped taking the pills?*

I'd already started to see myself break down emotionally. Were my focus and concentration and analytical skills next?

I dropped the handful of pills onto my bed and ran straight to Harry's room.

He was wearing headphones and had started a painting that was both garish and strangely familiar. The colors were swirled all around, but I could have sworn I recognized our father's face in the deep green, purple, and black shapes with striking white zigzags Harry was throwing onto the canvas.

I lifted one of his earpieces and said, "Harry—the pills. What are they for? Do you know?"

He shrugged. "You're the detective. I'm just an art dweeb."

"I think we should stop taking them."

"You do? But why?"

"Until we know what they are, I definitely think we should stop."

"What will happen?"

"I don't know for sure. But listen, Harry—we need to find out."

"But what if they're...necessary, or something? I've never *not* taken my pills. Malcolm and Maud would give us Big Chops for it."

"Malcolm and Maud are gone," I said, probably more harshly than I should have, because Harry's eyes began to water. "I just think we need to try this," I went on in a more soothing tone. "Don't you want to know what they're for...and why we are the way we are? I'm sure it's all connected somehow."

Harry looked at my doubtfully. Even in death our parents were still controlling him through their rules. "Okay," he finally said, smiling through his tears. "I'll stop being a druggie if you do."

"Good," I said, patting his hand and leaving him to his painting. We were one step closer to figuring everything out.

# 37

*The doorbell rang at* 7:26 the next morning, and this time I was ready for them. I wore jeans and a soft black cashmere turtleneck. I had brushed my hair, and I'd had coffee.

I opened the door and said to Caputo and Hayes, "What a surprise."

Caputo stepped around me and into the foyer. I flipped the light switch and the UFO blazed overhead and played the musical signature from Spielberg's *Close Encounters of the Third Kind.*

Hayes looked up at the light fixture and smiled. I was actually starting to like him a little. Not too much, though.

"Your parents must have been hilarious," he said.

I said, "Is this a social call? Or should I phone our lawyer?"

I didn't like the way-too-smug look on Caputo's face. Actually, I never liked his looks. At all.

"You should round up your brothers and your nanny," said Caputo. He didn't say please.

"Samantha is *not* our nanny."

"Whatever she is, just get her, Tinker Bell. We'll wait."

I called Philippe Montaigne. My call went to voice mail, so I left a message. Then I went down the hall to the bedroom wing. Since my uncle had issued a stern "do not disturb" order, I complied. My pleasure.

When my three brothers, Samantha, and I had assembled around the shark table, Caputo said directly to me, "We found fingerprints on the poison bottle, Tippytoes. *Your* prints."

My stomach dropped at the accusation, and my face felt hot. I wasn't sure my mouth would work properly. I had that disconcerting feeling of being out of control again.

None of my brothers said a word. Harry looked like he was about to cry again, and Hugo and Matthew just stared. *Thanks for the support, bros. Really appreciate it.*

Samantha looked shocked, too, but quickly opened her mouth to (I hoped) proclaim my innocence. I held up a hand and forced myself to speak instead.

"Are you seriously claiming that my prints are on the poison bottle? That's completely ridiculous."

"They're your prints, missy. Let's hear how they got on that bottle."

"If I actually *had* poisoned my parents, I would never make a dumb mistake like leaving my prints on the murder weapon. Trust me on that, dicks. No offense. That's slang for detective, isn't it?" This was something I never would have said forty-eight hours earlier. I wasn't sure I recognized myself anymore.

They just stared at me as I looked from one to the other of them. Then I got it.

"You don't have *any* fingerprints, do you?" I said. "That was a lie. You were trying to trap me because you have nothing. Having no evidence in the murders of a prominent couple like our parents is probably pretty embarrassing. Could hurt your careers."

Caputo said, "You're cute when you're mad, Tilly—"

"Tandoori!" I yelled at the same time that Matthew stood up, all 215 pounds of him. His arms were crossed over his chest and he stepped in front of me. As he did so, Samantha came to sit next to me on the couch.

"Anything else you want to falsely accuse my sister of, dicks?" Matthew said menacingly as he loomed over them.

---

with little terrors your own age."

Peck, you're a material witness and

That's officialese for *suspect*. May

chance to talk to us privately, yo

thoughts that will actually help us w

"Anyone too dumb to be afraic

promise: We're going to nail whoeve

Maud Angel, however many of you

you can count on that."

While Hugo jeered, I called Phil a

got his voice mail. I immediately re

eyes wide open with shock, as unbl

our pygmy sharks.

Phil still didn't answer.

Hugo had been running in circles

suddenly he stopped, climbed up on t

down his drawers, and mooned them

Hayes laughed.

Caputo said, "Get down from t

Your chariot awaits downstairs. In

paddy wagon."

They were really doing it.

*They were arresting our whole fa*

---

"You *can't take*

front of me, alon

and stood on N

busy imagining

like a snow gir

my scowl.

When I felt c

have I obstructe

Caputo said

winks."

Hayes stepp

playbook. "O

obstructs, imp

"Not so fast, |
Caputo said, stan
said, drawing ou
obstructing gove
degree. You're co

or prevents or attempts to preven
performing an official function by
physical force, or interference."

I rolled my eyes at him. "Yes, I
had listened to my question, you'd
obstructed you in the least."

Caputo said, "In your case, Tig
mention that your parents had a d
of the murders. And we're going t
ate omission with your refusal
investigation. Ditto for you, Harri

"Harrison!"

"You also omitted the dinner fr
as for you, Mr. NFL Rock Star, y
ing and interfering since you al
murders."

Matty scoffed. "You call wh
Please give me a chance to show y
tion." I swear I saw his muscles bu

Caputo and Matty stared at ea
against blue ice, until Hugo interr

"You've got nothing on me, |
hands off. I'm warning you."

"You're a material witness," sai
Shrimp Toast. Child Protective S

New York is one of only two states where the law treats
sixteen-year-olds as adults, not juveniles.

This was very bad news for Harry and me.

Caputo and Hayes personally drove us to the Manhattan Department of Correction, aka Central Booking.

"You're not going to separate us, are you?" Harry
croaked. He was so spent from all his crying that he looked
like a zombie, ghastly white.

"Take a guess, kid," Caputo replied.

I clutched Harry's hand for one last moment and said,
"Don't worry. Philippe will take care of us. I'll see you
soon."

And then I took a deep breath and readied myself for

what was next. *This should be interesting*, I told myself. *A study in our law-enforcement system, criminology at work.*

I was booked, given a baggy jumpsuit, and led down several steep flights of stairs, each step drawing me deeper into the hot, humid depths beneath the street. The walls of the prison were made of ancient-looking stone inset with iron gates. There were no windows. The whole place stank and was as dank as a dungeon.

It *was* a dungeon, actually, known throughout the city as "The Tombs."

I was jostled roughly into a small room, where Officer Frye, a blocky woman from Criminal Justice, waited to interview me.

"It's my job to determine if you're eligible for bail," she said with absolutely no inflection. "You can be held for up to three days until your arraignment."

*I could be here for* three days.

And then what would happen to me?

I answered her questions about my age and my circumstances, and told her that I had never been arrested before. I couldn't read Officer Frye's mind, but when she was satisfied, she went to the gate and called for the guards. Did she actually think I was dangerous?

Maybe I was. Maybe I am. *To put your foot through a*

*TV screen*, a voice inside my head pointed out, *you need superhuman strength—and deep, primal anger.*

And if I wasn't on drugs anymore—drugs that I suspected might have been taming my emotions—who knew what kind of anger I was capable of?

Two prison guards marched me from the interview room and down another flight of stairs, toward a large holding cell filled with drunks and jeering hookers. And then there was me—a sixteen-year-old under suspicion of matricide, patricide, and obstruction of governmental administration.

My brief feeling of superhuman power shrunk with every step I took. This was a dangerous place, and there was nowhere to hide. I crouched in a corner of the cell, covering my face with my hands.

# CONFESSION

*Why does this feel so…familiar?*

It's not the claustrophobia. My whole *world* is claustrophobic. Always has been. That's the life of an Angel.

It's not the grossly bad attitudes of the administrators, or the total foulness everywhere around me, either. I can handle this New York correctional facility dreck. *Tandy Angel is not frightened by jerk-off law enforcement trying to get media attention, right?* That's something I was raised to accept—that people will try to exploit us.

But there's something else that's ringing a bell, and it's making me anxious. Jittery. And it's getting worse and worse. Is it that I've not been taking my pills?

It's the air, I think. Something subtle in the smell, a smell you don't get *anywhere* in the day-to-day life of an elite Manhattan family. I can almost feel the olfactory receptors in my nose sending chemical signals to my brain, where the components are being lab-tested.

It's the smell of an institution. The smell of the unwell, and the smell that you use to cover that stink. And it's all mixed together with the reek of uncertainty, loneliness, and fear.

I haven't been in prison before... *have I?*

I'm getting a flash of memory now. I've been to a place *like* this before. I know it.

I have been institutionalized.

It feels shameful to say, but I have to say it. I have to start confronting it.

I was locked up for treatment. After he... was gone. Taken.

It was a place *my own parents* sent me to. A place where I was supposed to heal, but never totally did. A broken child is not something Malcolm and Maud knew how to handle.

So I stayed a little bit broken.

*Please, Philippe—anyone!—get me out of here.*

40

*It felt like an eternity before* I was extracted from the group cell and moved to a single cell for my safety. I felt sure Phil had done this somehow, and I loved him for it.

My private cell was as different from my bedroom in the Dakota as air is from ice. It was maybe five feet wide by six feet long, and furnished with a narrow, wooden slat for a cot. There was a toilet with no seat, and a caged fluorescent light outside my cell shot its death rays from high overhead.

Actually, things were looking up. At least I was alone.

I curled up on my sleeping board and at some point found myself thinking about the last time I had been left alone overnight in a dark, uncomfortable place. It was a chop in which I had to spend one night in the closet underneath the stairs. "Maybe you'll learn to appreciate the comforts we've provided for you if they're taken away," Malcolm said. "Maybe you'll reconsider your interest in so casually discarding the life that your mother and I have given you."

My interest in *discarding this life*—well, that's a topic worthy of another conversation.

I had always understood that our parents used reward and punishment to shape our characters. It was a dirty-dog shame that I'd gotten another Big Chop just hours before my parents died. I would never forget that they were angry and disappointed in me. If I had just kept my mouth shut, they might have left this earth with only good feelings about me in their hearts.

*That's if they actually* had *hearts, Tandy*, said the little voice in my head—which was getting a lot louder the more time I spent in that god-awful place.

*Of course they did*, I thought.

*Brains, yes. Hearts, debatable.*

Still, they really knew how to make people happy. I turned my mind to the last Grande Gongo I'd won, the previous year. It was a spectacular prize: a trip to the west coast of Australia, where I swam with whale sharks over the Ningaloo Reef.

The whale sharks were totally awesome—so gentle and huge. I drifted along with one I called Oliphant for almost an hour. He was about thirty-five feet long, with leopard spots and three hundred rows of tiny teeth, perfect for sieving plankton out of the sea.

I was a tiny speck in scuba gear, and Oliphant was a rare and wonderful behemoth, like a living flying carpet beneath me. Can you imagine it? Whatever you're imagining, double or triple it. That Grande Gongo was easily the highlight of my life.

My sister Katherine's Grande Gongo was also a highlight of her life—and the end of it, too.

*Katherine may not have been perfect* in my parents' eyes, but she was a perfect sister. Like her friends, she had a wild streak. She drank too much and had a secret boyfriend who was pierced and tattooed. And even though she lied to my parents—to everyone, really—and thought nothing of it (because she, too, was trained to not have much of a conscience), she was a true inspiration for me. I loved her so much.

Katherine was going to be an engineer and was only fifteen when she was admitted to MIT, probably the best university in the country for the next generation of top-flight scientists.

My parents were so overjoyed that they awarded her

the very first "Grande Gongo with an Asterisk." The asterisk meant that she could have or do anything with her Grande Gongo, without restriction.

Katherine wanted to harvest diamonds in the rough. What an adventure! She had a plan and a finely detailed map, and she said she'd be home in time for the start of school with enough diamonds to make a necklace that would light up a room. She promised me earrings and a ring. Harry wanted an earring, too.

After she turned sixteen she flew to South Africa, and within days she'd panned a large diamond from an alluvial mine. She sent us a picture of the stone, and it was a *whopper*—estimated at almost seven carats when cut, perfect for a solitaire or a pendant. And it certainly would have been a grand memento of the Grandest Gongo of them all.

Katherine also found a boyfriend in South Africa: Dominick. He was an older man, something that upset my father in particular. But Katherine told me all about him, and he wasn't a creepy pedophile type. He was just twenty-one, a free spirit, a beautiful boy, and they loved each other passionately.

I had always wondered what that would feel like. To love. Passionately. And in hours-long phone conversations and e-mail exchanges, I would ask Katherine to describe it. I wanted to know every little detail. I guess most people would say that what she told me was TMI, but I needed it. It was deeply fascinating to me.

Then, one horrible day, Dominick was driving a motorcycle, Katherine seated behind him with her arms around his waist. Suddenly he stopped, for no apparent reason. A bus rear-ended the bike, and my sister was thrown into the air. She was crushed under a speeding van coming from the opposite direction. Crushed, gone, extinct.

I have never really forgiven my parents for letting Katherine fly off on that fatal last Gongo. As smart as they were, they should have known her better, should have seen through her bravado and been less dazzled by her success.

Or maybe I should have told them what she was really like, that she was a wild child.

I have been haunted by the vision of my wonderful sister lying dead in the street every day since she died, just as I was that night in my prison cell.

Until that morbid image was hijacked by the sounds of hooting and banging on the iron bars of the jail.

It was just too much.

Tears welled in my eyes again and I bit down on my lip until it bled. There I was, trapped in that horrible place. A prime suspect in a double homicide. But I couldn't let my circumstances defeat me. My mind was still free, wasn't it?

I swore to myself, to my dead parents, and to my dear sister that if I had to, I would spend the rest of my life working to clear the Angel name.

I would find out who killed my mother and father.

And I would make whoever it was pay dearly.

# LOVE
## IN THE
# HOUSE OF ANGELS

# 42

*My incarceration was,* in some ways, a disconcerting metaphor for my whole life. I'd been raised in one of the most luxurious homes in Manhattan, and yet somehow I was seeing myself in the caged women surrounding me. There were even a few younger girls, like me, banging on the bars, screaming for dinner.

A guard in a green uniform came down the narrow tier pushing a food cart, shoving white-bread sandwiches through the slots in the iron bars.

When she got to me, she said, "How're you holding up?"

"Never better," I said.

"Court's over for the day. So take it easy. Try to sleep."

I ate my crap-cheese-and-mystery-meat sandwich and then lay down on my board. I wondered exactly which pill from Malcolm's pastel-colored assortment had produced the stumplike sleep that now eluded me.

I had a moment of desperate craving for those pills.

I swung wildly between being overwhelmed with emotion—and actually sort of liking the catharsis of it—and feeling like the pain of my situation was too much to bear.

A wave of self-pity hit me, and I wished more than anything that I were back in my room, watching the prisms in my windows bend the light into rainbows, listening to my parents move around in their suite upstairs.

*A pill could make this all go away*, I thought. *Like magic.*

I bit my hand so that I wouldn't cry and forced myself into an exercise I'd learned from Dr. Keyes that I thought might actually help me—the one she called FOF, or Focus on the Facts.

I concentrated and thought of everyone who lived in the Dakota, calling to mind the names and faces of every resident on every floor. I reviewed every insult I could remember, every grudge, and considered who among our neighbors might be a stealthy killer with a key.

I also considered each of my siblings as the possible murderer. I even wondered if *I* was the guilty party.

Was I a sleepwalking homicidal maniac? Could I have killed my parents and kept the terrible secret from myself? I'd been trained in burying trauma. Could I have poisoned them? What did I stand to gain? Or was it revenge?

Not revenge for having to do a Big Chop while standing on my head. I mean revenge for something else, something much bigger, something that maybe I don't remember.

Quick as lightning, a face flashed before my eyes. A boy's face. It gave me a warm feeling, then a painful one, then an angry one. Then it disappeared as fast as it came.

*FOF, Tandy.* I blinked three times just to make sure the face was really gone. *Focus on the Facts.*

And that boy, that face, that thing—it was just a ghost.

Or a demon.

# ⟨ CONFESSION ⟩

*I'm sure it was the good doctor* who made me forget the identifying details of that face. She must be the only one who understands why I can't seem to linger on its beauty long enough to really remember the person it belongs to. Why I can't study it long enough to understand the pain and anger I associate with it.

It took months of therapy, which Malcolm and Maud preferred to call "coaching," to get me to bury what started at the party that night, as well as everything that happened afterward—like, for instance, being institutionalized. If I hadn't been thrown in prison, I might never have remembered that.

Some days I worshipped Dr. Keyes for giving me sanity. Peace. And that very phlegmatic conscience. And sometimes I hated Dr. Keyes for it—as much as I was able to hate, anyway.

Allowing myself to feel pain would have been the one way to keep the boy behind the face alive in my heart.

I knew my transformation was complete when Dr. Keyes asked, "How are you feeling today, Tandy?" and I responded, "I'm not."

Freedom.

And by the way, my freedom wasn't exactly free. It cost about $250 an hour.

# 43

*I must have finally fallen asleep,* because I was totally confused when I woke up to the blare of a public-address system.

It was morning. And I was still in jail.

I sat up and scrubbed my face with my hands, then stretched my eyes wide open a couple of times.

Soon, Philippe would be coming to take me to my arraignment. I would face a judge, and I would be asked to say whether I was guilty or not, and the judge would determine if I would be tried for the murder of my parents.

I was taken to an interview room after breakfast— scrambled powdered eggs—had been served. Philippe arrived and greeted me with a shaky smile on his usually confident and handsome face.

He said, "The police have nothing on you, except that you were home when your parents were killed. The prints on the bottle are smudged, and the toxin is an unknown chemical that doesn't show up in the poison database."

"Are you getting me out of here, Philippe?"

"I talked to the DA. He doesn't like the obstruction charge. He thinks you could be found not guilty, and he'd rather try you for murder if the cops can put together a convincing case. So the DA told the cops to let you go."

I could hardly breathe. I said, "And my brothers?"

"They're being released, too, but I have to warn you, Tandy: The police won't give up. In fact, they're going to focus almost exclusively on those of you who were inside the apartment when your parents were killed."

# 44

*I changed into the clothes* Philippe had brought me, and then I was officially released. I was desperate to go home, but it wouldn't be easy to cut and run.

Philippe took me out through the correctional center's back door, and a roar went up from the mob of reporters who had gathered on the street. They were jamming the sidewalk right up to the face of the jail.

"Tandoori Angel!"

"Tandy, over *here*!"

"Look at me, Tandy!"

"Did you kill your parents? Did you kill them?"

The shouting *hurt*. It was a strange, uncomfortable sensation. A few days earlier, I'm sure I could have walked through this crowd hardly noticing the jeers, let alone feeling them. My parents had been dead for just three days, and now it felt like I was being assaulted with rocks.

Philippe put his hand at my back as a gigantic bouquet of microphones was shoved up to my face. I tried to make the statement Phil had coached me to say.

"I had nothing to do with my parents' deaths—"

My voice sounded like it belonged to a stranger as it echoed and bounced off the surrounding buildings. And before I could finish my prepared statement, I was pelted again with more fierce questions from rude people.

I got mad then. Hugo kind of mad. Matthew kind of mad. Kick-the-bejeesus-out-of-Robert kind of mad. I strangled the microphone in my grip.

"HEY!" I shouted with a sharpness I didn't recognize. The boom of my voice and the squeal of feedback washed over the reporters. A few of them put their hands over their ears, but they all gave me their full and quiet attention.

"I'm one of the victims!" I continued. "Do you *get* that? My parents are dead. If I were *your* child, would you act like this? I suppose you would, actually. You're all spineless. Rude. Barbarians. And of course you can quote me on that. Quote away."

The brief silence that followed my outburst was

shattered as all of the reporters began shouting at once. Philippe took the microphone from me and spoke to the mob.

"My client is innocent. The charges against the Angel children and Ms. Peck have been dropped. The entire family is cooperating fully with the police. We have no further comment at this time."

A pair of uniformed cops appeared beside me. One of them said, "This way, Miss Angel. Come this way." He actually seemed sort of nice as he reached out to take my arm and lead me inside, but I felt a little out of control and had to force myself not to push him away.

I did not want anyone to touch me. I just wanted to be with my family. What was left of it, anyway.

A dozen or so policemen linked arms and made a path for Philippe and me that would take us back into the relative safety of Central Booking. As I passed through the gauntlet, someone pinched my arm, *hard*. I yelped and turned in time to see a white-haired cop give me a cold smile.

He didn't have to say it. He thought I was a killer.

I glared at him so hard and felt so angry that I wondered if I might transform into a tiger or a werewolf, just like in those stupid movies. My mouth was as dry as cotton and my vision was starting to blur.

*So this is what fury is like.*

Philippe and I were swept through a series of doors to where Phil's car and driver waited between a Vietnamese take-out restaurant and a bail bondsman's storefront. I got into the backseat and rested my head against the window, trembling, overcome with weakness.

*You're experiencing withdrawal, Tandy*, that voice in my head said. *Face it: Your parents had you addicted to drugs.*

# 45

*I think I lost consciousness then* and didn't fully regain it until the car stopped in front of the Dakota.

Where we were met by more reporters.

Phil and his driver escorted me quickly through the crowd at the gates, inside the building, and into the elevator. Phil kept saying, over and over, "Don't let them rattle you, Tandy. You're going to be okay."

"Promise?"

Uncle Peter opened the front door to us, his face a mask of disapproval. I went into the living room but didn't see any sign of my brothers.

I was home. But home had never felt like this.

"Matthew is downtown with his slutty actress girl-friend," my uncle said. "Samantha is out looking for a rental apartment—and good luck to her. Harry is in bed. Hugo kicked a social worker in the shin. That was a mistake. He's currently buried under a few layers of bureaucracy."

My little brother was lost in the system? I wasn't worried that he might be scared, because Hugo isn't afraid of anything. But Hugo wouldn't recognize a dangerous situation if it sprouted claws and fangs and spewed fire through its nose.

Hugo would laugh out loud. And that scared *me*.

I went to his room and stood in the doorway, looking in at the broken bed, the unused toys, the stuffed pony and other relics of the childhood my little brother never really had.

I had to know if Hugo had anything to do with our parents' deaths. I just couldn't rule him out, and I needed to rule *somebody* out soon.

His computer was open on his desk, and I knew his password. I hadn't been sneaky; Hugo had told me what it was.

I touched the mouse and the computer jumped to life. I punched in *Ginats*, which is how Hugo spells *Giants*. Hugo has an IQ in the 160s, but he either can't or won't follow the rules of spelling.

I clicked open the file marked "H" and began to read my little brother's private journal. His early entries were bland and blameless, but as I scrolled down to the more recent entries, I found many mentions of our parents.

Hugo always called them "Malkim 'n' Mud."

*Tues. 4th. Malkim was ugly 2day. He had a big welt under his eye and a sour look. It was the real Malkim. No fool. He'z an ugly person + he'z not as smrty as he thinx.*

In similar entries about "Mud," Hugo described her as "batty" and "meen." It was clear that Hugo was sitting on a volcano of anger. I scrolled through his journal until I came to his entries for the previous summer.

Hugo had been only nine, but our parents' expectations were, of course, that he would bring home academic honors and that he wouldn't misbehave.

Despite warnings and Big Chops, Hugo consistently started fights with his classmates; he actually knocked out a total of three teeth, and was unabashedly proud of his right uppercut. He regularly muffed his homework and otherwise torpedoed his grades in courses he could have easily aced.

Last summer had been a bad one for Hugo.

For getting the lowest-possible grades and barely passing the fourth grade, Hugo was awarded a world-class Big Chop—and was sent far away from home.

# 46

*After Hugo was shipped out* for his draconian punishment, I interrogated Maud, and she finally relented and told me about Camp Kokopoki. After Hugo came home, he filled in the gaps between what Maud had said and the truth.

The camp was situated in the dead center of Maui, between ranches and rain forests, at the blackened base of a volcano. It was an army-style boot camp for out-of-control kids with a punishing regimen of predawn six-mile runs, grueling calisthenics, tasteless food, and big, bullying boys. And there were no phones, TVs, books, or iPads—none of the comforts that most of us take for granted these days.

When he wasn't doing paramilitary drills, Hugo was attached to a farm detail, where he worked among prickly pineapple plants, weeding and harvesting in the broiling heat of the Hawaiian sun. He cut his hands, got a scalding sunburn, and acquired colonies of blisters.

Have I mentioned that he was only nine?

Our parents knew what Hugo would go through there, and they approved. They wanted him to learn about the rule of law and to appreciate the soft life he had in New York City. I wonder if they ever considered that forced obedience just might make Hugo murderous....

I scrolled to Hugo's first journal entry—made when he got home from Maui. He had written:

*I hate Malkim and Mud. I want them to dye.*
*They would totally deserve it.*

I had to read the sentence a few times to make sure that I'd read it right, and when I did a search for the words *dye*, *dyed*, and *dead*, I found that Hugo had wished for our parents' deaths several times:

*I wouldn't care if they dyed.*
*They should be dead.*

*Malkim and Mud are monsters, human*
  *monsters. Dye monsters, dye.*

I took a deep breath. After reading Hugo's journal, it wasn't so hard for me to imagine him mixing up a poison and giving it to our parents to drink before bed. They might have humored him, thinking they were making peace with their little boy.

I wanted to see him. To look into his eyes. To ask him to tell me that he hadn't killed Malkim 'n' Mud.

If he told me he was innocent, would I believe him?

# CONFESSION

*You probably wonder how I could* even consider a ten-year-old boy as a possible suspect, don't you?

Maybe you've never seen a six-year-old gleefully hack at a teddy bear with a butcher knife.

*Boys will be boys*, you say? You think Hugo was just playing a game of knights and ninjas?

Unlikely. If Hugo were playing knights, he'd be wearing the complete set of armor (made out of tin) that Malcolm had custom-made by the costume shop at the Metropolitan Opera. If he were playing ninja, he'd be wearing his junior-sized balaclava and using his replica samurai sword.

Instead, he was a hundred percent Hugo, Spider-Man pj's and all. He slashed and sawed at the teddy bear he and Maud had just built together at the Build-A-Bear Workshop for his birthday. He called the bear Malcolm.

And he laughed and laughed and laughed.

He was already a sociopath, and he was just out of kinder-garten.

I didn't think much of it at the time. It was the family way.

# 47

*Could you ever spy on your own family* the way I spied on mine? Could you, if you thought somebody in your house was a murderer? Don't be too sure about how you'd react to things you haven't actually experienced. You might be a little surprised by what you're capable of.

I was closing down Hugo's computer when the intercom screeched and Harry's voice filled all nine thousand square feet of our apartment.

*"Calling Tandy. Calling Tandy.* Are you home? Meet me in the kitchen, stat."

Harry sounded borderline hysterical. I am not kidding.

The kitchen was like a mile from Hugo's room, but I

ran, slid into the kitchen on socked feet, and found Harry staring at the small under-cabinet television set.

"Look at *this*," he said, hitting the rewind button on our DVR.

"Well, hello to you, too, Harry. Glad you made it out of jail. I'm just fine. Thanks for asking."

"Of course you're fine, Tandy. You're always fine," he replied. He paused, then said, "I'm glad you're home. Now *look*!"

It was a breaking news report by someone called Laurie Kim, a young, ambitious TV reporter sitting eagerly behind the anchor desk. Behind her perky face was a full-screen video of Matthew making a touchdown on the Giants' home field.

"What's this about?" I asked.

"Watch," Harry whispered.

The reporter was saying, "Tamara Gee, the actress best known for her starring role in *The Good Girls* and for her love relationship with football star Matthew Angel…"

Laurie Kim continued her celebrity-reporter-style blather as the screen behind her cut to footage of the stands, where Tamara Gee cheered as players carried Matthew off the field on their shoulders.

"…But you can't always judge a relationship by its

appearance. Earlier today, I had an exclusive interview with Ms. Gee in the apartment she shares with her 'Matty.' "

The producers cut to another video clip, this one of Tamara Gee speaking with Ms. Kim in a perfectly decorated living room with plump pillows in tropical colors.

Tamara's beautiful face was positively aglow when she said, "I don't want to deny it any longer. I am pregnant with my first child, and he is an Angel. The baby's father is Malcolm Angel, the man I loved—the man who was just *murdered*." Her face contorted in what I immediately identified as well-rehearsed grief.

A photo of my father appeared in the corner of the screen as Ms. Kim asked, "Just to be sure we all understand, you're saying that Matthew Angel is not the baby's father?"

"That's right. *Malcolm* Angel was my lover, and he is my baby's father. Sadly, my child will never know his daddy."

My hands flew to my head as I screamed, "*Hold it!* This is complete *crap*. I don't even under*stand* it. She's saying Malcolm fathered her *child*. That he *cheated* on Maud? With *her*? That's a lie. It can't be true."

"I don't believe it," Harry said, his voice faint. His face looked positively ashen.

"She's a liar, and we need to call Philippe right now," I said.

"Why would she lie?" Harry asked me.

If she was lying, it was a crime against my father. Defamation. If she was telling the truth, and my father had cheated on my mother with Tamara Gee, it was a crime against our family, and a double crime against poor Matty.

"I can think of about a hundred million reasons, but only one that matters," I said. "Money. That's usually the reason for almost everything adults do, isn't it?"

"Yeah, but…I can't…quite…absorb…all this…." Harry was starting to go white again. "I've got to call Matty…."

He started to pull out his phone, but I stopped him, suddenly remembering my visit with Mrs. Hauser two days earlier.

"Harry, listen to this. Mrs. Hauser heard Malcolm and Maud fighting the day they died. Malcolm was saying he wanted to make some 'new financial arrangements.' And Maud was really mad."

"New financial arrangements? Like…for a certain incoming member of the family? You've got to be kidding me," said Harry.

If Tamara and Malcolm really were involved—and the

very thought of it nearly made me gag—Matthew had an undeniable motive to commit murder. It would be called a crime of passion.

To be perfectly honest, I find that phrase a little incomprehensible. I mean, I get it—but I don't really get it.

# CONFESSION

*There's a famous phrase from Shakespeare* you might have heard at some point: *The lady doth protest too much, methinks.*

That was me, saying this horror couldn't be true. Because you know what? I really wasn't sure that Tamara was lying. At all.

After all, there had to be a concrete reason I'd never trusted Tamara; I generally don't react to people emotionally. I analyze them.

At the same time I was accusing Tamara of lying, an image flashed into my mind. Setting: our kitchen. Suspects: my father and Tamara Gee. Malcolm is leaning in toward Tamara, gently nudging her against the fridge…or maybe she is pulling him against her; I can't be sure. What I *am* sure of is that there were no unwilling participants in this affair.

If you saw your father whispering sweet nothings into the ear of your brother's girlfriend, and if you saw her giggle in response and nuzzle your father's face and neck, and if you saw him smile and laugh and basically encourage the whole disgusting exchange, it would freak you out, right?

What would you do? Would you pretend you didn't see it and just barge in, saying, "Excuse me, I need to get into the fridge!" Or would you say, "What the hell are you *doing*?" Would you hold them accountable for their actions? Would you turn around and quietly leave? Would you tell your brother?

I didn't know what to do. And thanks to Dr. Keyes and her great skill in teaching us to shatter our crippling memories, the flicker of this particular memory is so faded and gray, I'm not certain it ever actually happened. I could easily have dreamed it.

And since I will only ever act on the facts, I'm sure I never told Matthew.

But...I *should* have, shouldn't I?

# 48

*Harry looked beaten down.* Actually, *stomped* might be a better word. As if Matthew's football-playing teammates had used him as the playing field.

He took a carton of milk out of the fridge and poured himself a drink with a shaking hand, sloshing the liquid over the glass, onto the counter and the floor. Harry stared at the puddle of milk as if it might be the one tiny thing that would finally break him completely—the last straw, as they say.

He took his inhaler out of his pocket and sucked at the mouthpiece. Then, with a wheeze in his voice, he said, "Last night. It was like trying to sleep in hell."

"At least hell would have been warmer," I said, remembering the cold of my cell.

"I didn't sleep the night before, either. Did you?"

"In thirty-second winks, between hours and hours and hours of staring up at the ceiling."

"I'm taking this," Harry said, holding up a square red pill. He tossed it back and chased it with the milk. Then he said, "I'm going to bed now, and no one had better bother me, because if I don't sleep I'll go over the edge. And I might not come back."

"Which pill is that?" I asked sharply.

"Angel Pharma's red pill for sleep and sweet dreams. I think it's hibiscus. You want one?"

I was sorely tempted. Suddenly I became aware that my hand was starting to shake. Life was easier on the pills, somehow. And sleep sounded like such a heavenly, peaceful escape from this nightmare....

But no. I needed to meet Tandoori Angel—the real one. The one who wasn't molded, beaten down and perked up, and supernaturally enhanced by drugs.

"I want to get off the pills," I forced myself to say. "All of them. And you should, too. I thought you told me you were quitting."

"What, do you want *me* to die, too, Tandy? Like our

parents? Because I'm telling you, I can't live without sleep right now."

I resisted the urge to slap him, an urge I'd never felt before. I hated it. Hated it. Was this the real Tandy?

I decided to go back to the Tandy I knew. FOF Tandy.

"Tamara Gee's probably lying," I said, changing the subject.

"Actually, I believe her," Harry said. He put up a hand, then coughed and coughed, trying to get a good breath. After his coughing fit, he set his empty glass on the counter and slouched out of the kitchen.

"Sleep like a stump," I called after him.

I hit the rewind button on the DVR and watched Laurie Kim's interview with Matty's so-called girlfriend, Tamara Gee, again. It was impressive. Tamara made good eye contact with Ms. Kim. She didn't fidget. She looked confident—and truthful.

But Tamara Gee is an actress.

She could probably lie convincingly about how many thumbs she has. And if she was lying about being pregnant with my father's baby, the only reason that made sense was that she hoped to land a big settlement from the over-stuffed Angel estate.

And then a new thought came to me, like a train pulling

into Grand Central Terminal: Had my mother known of this affair? If she knew, she would have borne the pain—and hidden it completely, of course—in order to keep our family intact and avoid public humiliation.

Maud had few friends, but she had a confidante in her assistant, Samantha Peck. If Maud had known about Malcolm and Tamara, she might have told Samantha.

And Samantha had, after all, told me that my mother was a woman of many secrets....

Was this one of them?

I was going to try to find out.

# 49

*Not only was Samantha intelligent,* but I truly believed she genuinely liked my mother. If Maud had told Samantha that my father was having an affair, Samantha would have kept her confidence as a matter of principle.

I left the kitchen and went down the hall to Samantha's room. I knocked, and when she didn't answer the door, I turned the knob, entered her very organized room, and got to work.

Half of the space was a tidy pink bedroom; the other half was an efficient little office with a bank of file cabinets, a wooden desk that held a laptop and a printer, and a swivel desk chair.

I was not surprised to find that the computer was password-protected and my random guesses wouldn't get me in.

Aside from the computer and printer, there were only a few items on Samantha's desk: a heavy-duty stapler, a set of Russian nesting dolls, and a crystal bowl filled with peppermint candies.

I unwrapped a peppermint and sucked on it as I opened the desk drawer.

Apparently Samantha liked little boxes, as the top drawer was full of them: candy tins, enameled pillboxes, porcelain heart-shaped containers, and a sturdy little box made of stone.

Inside the stone box was a bunch of small keys. Was this *it*? Far too easy. Working quickly, I opened the thirty file drawers, one at a time. What were my mother's secrets? Would there be a record of them here?

I thumbed through a lot of files filled with paid bills, memos, and tax returns. I found receipts for furniture and for artwork, and I came across a file of birthday cards from all of us kids to Maud. I thought it was uncharacteristically sentimental of her to have saved them.

I spotted my self-conscious nine-year-old handwriting in one card:

*Dearest Mother,*

*Happy Birthday. May you find today productive and fulfilling. I will spend the day working on my Latin and learning how to construct the perfect birthday cake with Father. We will all enjoy it together when you come home.*

*Sincerely, Tandoori*

Even *I* could tell that was not normal. Not in the least.

Then I found a whole standing file case relating to my mother's company, as well as full drawers concerning Royal Rampling, the man who was suing Maud. Did he have an interest in seeing my mother dead? It was certainly my investigative responsibility to study these files in painstaking detail.

But I wasn't ready to do that yet. Please don't ask me why.

Instead, my fingers started nervously flipping through the folders, my eyes scanning faster and faster until I got to the back of the bottom drawer. I halted when I spotted some familiar writing. I recognized it as having come from my own hand. The folder was labeled J.R.

Did I want to look at this?

*Yes, Tandy*, a little voice told me. *Go ahead.*

I can't call what was in front of me "my" handwriting per se, because it was done in calligraphy. At least a hundred pages, all written with an old-fashioned flat-nib pen and a bottle of ink. I'd copied the more than ten thousand words of Alfred, Lord Tennyson's famous poem "Maud." In Germanic gothic script. It had been a wicked Big Chop, I remember that much.

But for what? The whole point of a Big Chop was to make certain that you would never, ever again make the mistake you made to merit the chop.

What had I done to deserve this specific punishment?

I wasn't ready to go back to that place yet.

I quickly flipped through the first fifty pages, scanning the poem. Many of the words themselves chilled me: *"Villainy somewhere! Whose? One says, we are villains all...."* But what chilled me even more was remembering how I'd felt when I wrote those words: like a traitor.

Shivers started shooting up and down my spine to the point that I felt nearly paralyzed.

I shut the folder and slammed it back into the drawer.

*Not now, Tandy. This is distracting you from the real mystery*, I reminded myself. *Leave it alone.*

# 50

*Despite all the searching,* I discovered nothing concerning Malcolm and Tamara's alleged affair. I threw myself into Samantha's chair, propped my feet up on her desk, and took a long look around the room.

My detecting instincts were telling me that I was missing something important here about Malcolm and Maud's relationship.

I was, I was, I was—until I *wasn't.*

As I swiveled in Samantha's chair, my shoe hit the desk, which shook the egg-shaped set of Russian nesting dolls. The toy tipped over and rolled toward the edge of the desk, but I managed to grab it before it fell. Then I gave it a closer look.

Like many nesting dolls, this set was wooden, hollow, and brightly painted to look like a Russian peasant woman. It was made so that the outer doll could be taken apart to reveal the next, smaller doll inside. The largest, outermost doll had a painted red scarf. The next doll inside held a bouquet of daisies.

I kept opening the successively smaller dolls until I was holding the sixth and smallest one. I shook it and heard something rattle inside that didn't sound like another doll. It sounded metallic. Another key?

I twisted open the smallest doll and found a folded paper. And inside the paper was a lump of gold.

I pulled out the lump and straightened out a delicate gold chain that held a heart-shaped locket with a brilliant-cut center diamond.

I turned on the desk lamp, then opened the locket.

Inside was a tiny snapshot of my mother and Samantha, both of them smiling broadly.

I had to squint to read the inscription on the back of the locket, but it was legible.

SAMMY, LOVE FOREVER—MAUD

My heart banged inside my chest like a racehorse trying to kick down its stall.

What was *this*?

*Sammy, love forever—Maud.*

My mother wasn't an air-kisser. She would never say "love forever" casually. I don't remember my mother ever telling *me* that she loved *me*.

I held the locket in my sweating hand and tried to make sense of the new shape my ideas were taking. My mother and "Sammy." Love forever.

Was my mother actually having a love affair with Samantha? How could I not have known, with both of them living under this roof? And was this why my father might have had an extramarital affair of his own?

Or had Maud and Samantha's bond been strengthened, even transformed, after my mother learned of my father's dalliance with a woman young enough to be his daughter?

It didn't matter. At that moment, all I could see was that both of them were traitors. And liars. To each other, to their family. To me.

No wonder they were both dead.

It was starting not to seem so very shocking anymore.

# 51

*The first thing I did was* wake up Harry.

Harry didn't like being woken up one bit, of course. He shoved me aside and pulled the covers over his head. "Go away, Tandy. Get *out* of here. I'm *not kidding.*"

"I'm sorry, but YOU HAVE TO SEE THIS!"

I yanked down the blankets and opened one of his eyes with my fingers.

He batted my hand away. "Are you crazy?"

"Look at this, then you tell me."

I switched on the light next to Harry's bed and gave him the locket.

I bit down hard on my lip as he opened the heart and

looked at the picture. Then Harry did as I had done; he flipped the locket over and read the inscription.

He read the engraving a second time, then handed me the locket, fell back onto his pillow, and pulled the covers over his face again.

I poked his arm. "So, what do you think?"

"Think? I can't think anymore. I can only feel pain. What is going *on* around here? I mean, what *was* going on?"

*Focus on the facts, Tandy.* "*Both* our parents were probably having affairs. Only Maud's looks like was going on inside our *home*." I swallowed. "That's pretty sad."

"Sad? I call it sick! I call it outrageously disrespectful to every other Angel in the house."

"Well, I call Malcolm screwing around with a girl young enough to be my sister—who is ALSO MY BROTHER'S GIRLFRIEND!—probably even more outrageously sick and disrespectful."

"That, too," said Harry. "Let's face it, our 'rents were pretty despicable. No wonder they're dead."

My thoughts were blooming like poisonous flowers, bright and noxious and irrepressible.

"Harry, think about this. I'm just trying out a theory, okay? What if Samantha wanted to go public with the love affair? What if she wanted Maud to leave Malcolm? What if Maud refused? People have been killed for less rejection than that."

"Be careful, Tandy. All you have to support this theory is an inscription on a locket."

"It's a lead. It's a clue."

"We've got to trust Samantha until we know that we can't."

"Trust?" I narrowed my eyes. "That's not something that makes a whole lot of sense right now, Harry. The only person I trust at this moment"—I paused to think about it—"is you."

"Gee, thanks for the vote of confidence."

I pulled out my phone and dialed Samantha's number.

"I'm right around the corner," she told me. "I'll be home in five or six minutes."

Harry and I were waiting for her when she came through the door, looking oh-so-pretty in pink.

"Tandy! I'm so glad you're back," she said, wrapping me in a huge hug. "Are you okay? Did Philippe bring you home? I can't imagine you trapped in that terrible place!" She finally let me go and stepped back to look at our faces. "Oh, dear. What's wrong now?" she asked as she set her Hermès bag on the floor.

"Please join us, Samantha," I said. "Harry and I have a question that only you can answer."

*Did you kill our mother and father?*

# 52

Samantha had also spent the previous night in The Tombs. She had since washed her hair and changed her clothes, but there were inky circles under her eyes, as if she'd stood with her back to the wall all night, fearing for her life.

Which was okay with me. According to what I knew of police practices and procedures, a suspect under pressure was a suspect more likely to tell the truth.

And I would accept nothing less.

When Samantha sat down in the living room, I held up the locket, letting it swing so that light bounced off the diamond.

"I found this in your room," I said. "Recognize it? I'm sure you do. The inscription says 'Sammy, love forever—

Maud.' That's pretty mushy for my mother. In fact, it's so unlike her that I'd like you to tell me what she meant."

"I don't like your tone, Tandy. It's none of your business, and furthermore, it was very, very wrong of you to pry into my personal things."

"This is one of those situations where the ends justify the means, don't you think, 'Sammy'?"

Samantha heaved a long sigh. She tilted her head back and stared at the ceiling over the fireplace until I said, "Well?"

"Okay, Tandy, okay. You're right," Samantha said. "Your mother and I…had a relationship. It just *happened*…and both of us were taken by surprise. But the longer it went on, the more we realized we loved each other."

"There's a difference between loving each other and being in love." I was surprised by the authority with which I said it. Katherine had told me that once, I guess. "Which was it?"

"We were in love," Samantha said. "We never wanted any of you kids to know."

"I'm going to run away and join the circus," Harry said to his shoes. "Wait—I already live in the circus."

I pressed Samantha. "Who knew about your relationship? Did Malcolm know you were involved with my mother, *Sammy*? Did you know anything about my father and Tamara Gee?"

"I found a great place to live," Samantha said, changing the subject. She swept her long hair back with her hands. "It's a studio on Ninety-second and Amsterdam. I can see you whenever you like. I can babysit Hugo. I'd like to do that, actually—"

"What were your plans before the murder?" I asked her. "Yours and Maud's?"

"We didn't have any *plans*. Hugo is still young. We would never have done anything to hurt anyone. Please don't ask me any more questions, Tandy. I'm grieving. I feel gutted. I don't expect you to understand or even to care, but please respect what I'm going through. To be quite honest, I'm the only one here who's really lost someone they deeply loved."

*Ouch.* I resisted the strange and sudden temptation to slap her. *I know what it feels like to lose someone you love. How dare you…*

Then: Deep breath in through the nose. Out through the mouth.

"Actually," I said calmly, and the words sounded and felt strange even as they were coming out of my mouth, "I do care."

As if on cue, Hugo came through the front door, with

Philippe Montaigne right behind him. Hugo had on the same clothes he'd been wearing when we were sent to jail: cut-off jeans and an orange LIFE IS GOOD T-shirt with the secondary slogan ENJOY THE RIDE. He also had a black eye.

Phil said, "He ran away from the unsecured detention in Midtown and went looking for Matthew. The police found him sleeping on the grass in Bryant Park."

"I'm *starving*," Hugo said, grinning as only a ten-year-old can. "I could eat an alligator. The whole thing. By myself."

I had to agree with Harry. I did already live in the circus. And it was a five-ring affair.

# 53

*Hugo wasn't the only one who was hungry,* so we went to Shun Lee West, our favorite restaurant in the neighborhood. Once there, we sprawled in the black leather embrace of our usual booth. We'd even invited Samantha, and honestly, I *did* care about her feelings.

Matthew met us there, and I was stunned to see my handsome brother's face so tired, his eyes so dull. The news about Tamara had clearly shocked him, and it seemed that the media glare was getting to him. Harry and I hugged him even harder than we had after our parents died.

Twenty minutes later, Hugo was cramming spicy Sichuan alligator into his mouth. He was very happy now. He was the only one who was.

The familiar place, the routine, and the comfort food were just a cover for our seething anxiety. We were all out of jail, but we were not free by any means. As Philippe had told me, Sergeant Caputo was taking this case personally, for some reason I couldn't understand. He wasn't going to give up.

I wasn't giving up, either.

In fact, I had a new agenda.

Having dinner with my siblings and Samantha gave me the opportunity to question everyone at once. Maybe I could persuade or trap someone into making a confession.

Matthew sucked down his third glass of Tsingtao beer, then said, "I overheard a couple of cops saying they think we did it together, that the murders were a conspiracy."

"Some people think *you* did it," said Hugo. "I know how people get pregnant—duh—and if Malcolm did that to your girlfriend, that must have made you really, *really* mad."

Matty smiled wanly at Hugo, and tousled his hair, but remained silent.

I waited as the server refilled our water glasses, then said, "At this point, family secrets could take *all* of us down. Matty, I know you don't want to talk about this, but I think it's fair to ask you to clear up this story. Is Tamara pregnant? By"—I gulped—"Malcolm?"

Hugo and Harry gagged a little. I didn't blame them. Samantha pressed her lips together in a pained expression of distaste.

My brother fixed me with his bug-eyed stare. "How am I supposed to know? I haven't seen any DNA test. I didn't know she was pregnant until I saw her on the *news*. Can you believe that? I *still* don't know anything. She's not at the apartment. She won't answer her phone."

I knew this hurt Matty, but my weakly developed conscience allowed me to press on with the questioning. I practiced stating the horrible facts without any emotion whatsoever.

"Matty, please answer the question. *Was Tamara sleeping with Malcolm?*" Gags rippled around the table again. "There's no way Tamara told the channel six news and didn't tell you."

"Really? And how well do you know *Tamara*?" Matthew shouted at me. "How do you know what psycho *ideas* she gets? And here's another question, Tan-*doori*: Who appointed you Lord High Executioner?"

Samantha put her hands to her face. "Calm down, everyone. Calm down." Her voice wobbled.

And then she fell apart.

"I miss Maud so much," she cried.

We all looked at Samantha, who was now bawling noisily. Oh, geez. It was bad. All of it, all the time.

"Hey, hey," I said. "Please don't cry."

Samantha only cried harder.

Just then, a hush sucked the ambient sound right out of the restaurant. I looked up and saw that nearly all the other diners were staring at us.

Hugo dropped his fork, flicked his eyes back and forth, and then said in a really loud voice, "Haven't you people ever seen someone cry before?"

The stares continued for a moment, until a bald guy in a plaid jacket started to laugh. A few more people joined in; apparently they found this scene hilarious. I didn't see anything funny about it, though, and Hugo must've felt the same way, because he stuck his pinkie fingers in his mouth and whistled for attention.

When he got it, he flipped the bird at the bald guy.

Harry grinned.

Then *Harry* gave everyone in the restaurant the finger, and then so did Matthew. I couldn't be left out of this, so my middle finger went up, too. Samantha dabbed at her eyes, then joined us in flipping off the diners at Shun Lee.

Five middle fingers.

We all laughed hysterically, out of control. The server rushed over to Matthew, brandishing the check, basically begging us to leave, and we were all overcome by another bout of uncontrollable laughter.

You have to take your yuks where you can find them, right? Especially if the justice system wants to hang you and your sibs for murder.

# 54

*It was way after midnight,* and the only light in the apartment came from the glowing green of the sharks' phosphorescent bodies. Everyone was asleep but me.

The writer Colette once wrote, "There are days when solitude is a heady wine that intoxicates you with freedom, others when it is a bitter tonic, and still others when it is a poison that makes you beat your head against the wall." I felt like I'd been beating my head against the wall for four days almost to the minute.

I was next to nowhere in my investigation. There was virtually no evidence, there were no known witnesses, and because my parents had at least a couple hundred million dollars, anyone in line to inherit had a motive to kill. And there were a lot of us. None of us could be counted out. Not even me.

I pulled a chair up next to Robert and switched on the lamp behind him, which illuminated Harry's new painting of Malcolm and Maud, hanging above Robert's TV. He called it *What Love Looks Like*, and he'd depicted our parents in acid green and bloody purple, their arms around each other and their mouths open in silent screams as they confronted the viewer with their stares.

Harry had remarked to me as he hung it: "Our parents were gods and monsters at the same time. Maybe we're all like that—gods and monsters."

Harry's use of extreme light and dark colors allowed for multiple and opposite interpretations of the work, as he'd intended, but in my humble opinion, Harry had deemphasized our parents' godlike traits while capturing their more monstrous qualities with real feeling.

Maud might have liked this painting, because there was nothing sentimental about it. The style was abstract and expressionistic; it reminded me of Picasso's weird distortions and Francis Bacon's gruesome imagery.

Harry's latest work evoked a very strong emotion in me, attractive and repulsive at the same time. As I stared at the painting, that emotion swelled, and my head started to spin.

What was happening? Was it the drug withdrawal?

And then I hallucinated again. I thought I saw that face, a bit clearer this time. He was handsome....No. More than that. Deeply attractive. And yet—somehow repellant to me at the same time...

I felt a sudden heaving in my chest, so forceful that I stood up and clutched my heart just to make sure I wasn't in cardiac arrest.

The ghostly face was gone, but I staggered over to the painting that had triggered the frightening response and snatched it from its hanger.

A nail fell to the floor.

Too easily, as though it had been hammered right through the wall and into an empty space on the other side.

Suddenly, I refocused back on the mystery. Setting the painting down, I remembered the closet on the other side of the wall.

Years earlier, I had seen my father coming out of that closet. When I asked him about it, he told me that he and

Maud stored their out-of-season clothing there. And then he locked the door.

I was twelve at the time, old enough to register my father's strange expression. But I was in middle school, and closets were pretty low on my list of interests.

But now? My father's secret hiding place had just shot up to the number one position.

I left the living room and moved along the corridor behind the stairs. I stopped where I had seen my father emerge from the closet.

It was the same closet where I'd spent my sleepless night as a Big Chop.

The police had broken off the lock and looked through the closet, as they'd done everywhere in the apartment, but they hadn't found anything. Then again, they were obviously incompetent.

You see, during that night that I wasn't allowed to lie down, I'd had time to really search the closet for the secret I knew must be inside. Why else would my father have a lock on a closet door? Why else would he look so strange when he came out of the closet? After hours of looking, I had finally found a door that blended so seamlessly into the wall, you'd never see it without spending hours examining every crack.

Had my father wanted me to find it? I guess I'd never know. It didn't matter, though, because the door hadn't budged that night, and I still couldn't find a way to make it budge.

But there had to be a key somewhere in this house. And I was going to find it.

# 55

*My feet hardly touched the treads* as I ran up the stairs to my parents' suite. I dialed up the hallway lights, and even in the pale glow coming from the hall, their room looked blasted and horrifying.

I stood on the threshold, cold sweat beading up all over my body. I actually started to shake. Before I could stop it, my mind had called up the horrific image of my parents' twisted bodies on the bed.

I felt sick at the thought that they had been betrayed by someone they knew and trusted.

What were they thinking before they died? Did they even know who had murdered them?

Had they tried to save themselves?

I gripped the doorjamb with both hands until my rapid heartbeat slowed. Then I took a tentative step forward and entered my parents' room. The place where they made babies, the place where they made *me*.

This most private of rooms had been frozen in the aftermath of the chaos. Belongings had been dumped from dresser drawers and lay in a jumble on the floor. Dead flowers drooped in a vase on the fireplace mantel, and the armoire doors were opened wide, as if they were pleading with me to come in and find the truth.

I was determined to stay until I found it.

After checking out the mantel and the tops of the bedside tables, I went to my parents' walk-in closet.

My father's clothing was bunched along the rod on the left side, and my mother's clothes were crushed together on the right. Designer garments had fallen off hangers and were lying in glittering heaps on the floor.

I went to work.

I frisked every pocket, each article of clothing sending up a flurry of good and bad memories as I touched it: a vintage Chanel suit Maud had worn when she'd taken Katherine and me to the ballet; a coat Father had worn on a snowy day when the bunch of us had played touch football in the park. I'd almost forgotten that day, but the sudden memory of playing football with Matthew sent a rare feeling of warmth through me.

I seized on the jacket my mother used to throw on over her jeans—a sexy, sparkly, spangled navy-blue thing that had once belonged to Madonna.

I put it on and smelled Maud's ylang-ylang fragrance. My eyes filled with tears, and a few of them spilled over. Maud had loved this jacket. She looked ten years younger when she wore it, maybe because it made her feel ten years younger. She'd never let me wear it. The fact that I could just slip it on now without fearing her wrath made me feel a strange sort of ache inside.

I looked at myself in my mother's mirror—and I saw a dead girl walking. My eyes were dark and sunken. My hair was lank in my headband. I looked like Alice after she'd taken a tour of Wonderland's meatpacking plant.

*Do not dissolve into mush, Tandy. Do not go there. Come back to the living, bucko.*

I put the brakes on my useless trip down memory highway and left the closet. I sifted through the piles of clothing and other miscellany on the bedroom floor. The police had started throwing things into haphazard piles once they'd determined which items should be confiscated. Littered among the sweaters and undergarments were foreign coins, a packet of letters to my father from Gram Hilda, and a gold rattle that had belonged to Harry—but no key to my father's closet.

I ran my hand behind the flag painting and then, before going through the stack of books on the floor, turned on the light next to my father's side of the bed.

The lamp is French, an electrified oil lamp from the nineteenth century, made of bronze with a glass ball shade. Its style is seriously at odds with our modern décor. But Gram Hilda gave it to my father, and he loved his mother despite how she'd hurt him. Or maybe because of it? In any case, her gift lit up his bedside every night of his life. On a hunch, I carefully lifted the glass shade and gently shook it.

A key fell out onto the bed.

I stared at it for a few long seconds. Could it really be that easy?

It was just past two in the morning. Time to wake up my twin again.

I knocked on Harry's door until I heard him groan, then went inside and shook him awake.

"Gah, Tandy. What is *wrong* with you? What *time* is it, anyway?"

"You've noticed Malcolm's closet?"

"What? Which closet?"

"The one under the stairs."

"The police didn't find anything in it. Now *go away*. Come back at noon. At the earliest."

I held up the key, just visible in the light beaming through Harry's window from the city that never sleeps.

"I think this is important. You have to come with me."

# 56

*I had started to shiver again,* maybe because I was afraid I might actually solve this mystery soon.

I opened the closet door, turned on the light, and walked over to where I remembered finding the door. It took me a few minutes to locate it again.

"Tandy, what are you doing?" Harry asked, shivering a little himself. He sat on an old suitcase near the door.

"There's something here. I just have to figure out how to open it," I replied. I felt around the outline of the door. Could I have just imagined it? Maybe it was nothing. I put my face up against the cold wall and looked closely at every tiny bump, searching for anything that looked uneven. That's when I saw the tiny slot.

"I knew it!" I crowed. Harry looked startled, but he approached as I slipped the key into the slot and turned it. I pushed open the door.

And I was shocked to the core, as if I'd stuck my worst expectations into a water-soaked light socket.

"Tandy…what is this?" Harry asked, peering inside.

This was no secret closet. It was a secret room, maybe fifteen feet long and five or six feet wide, with a low, slanted ceiling. It was lined with built-in cabinetry and countertops that were crammed with beakers and scales and computer equipment. I saw what seemed to be a centrifuge in one corner.

It was astounding, beyond the limits of my imagination. This hidden room was a *laboratory*.

Old Victorian buildings like the Dakota sometimes have eccentric architecture, and odd rooms-behind-rooms are often walled off during renovations. But Malcolm had preserved this, the forgotten space under the stairs.

"Am I hallucinating?" I asked Harry. Given how strange I'd been feeling and acting since my parents' deaths, I thought there was a fair chance that I was.

"If you're tripping, then both of us are," Harry replied. "I believe we've found Dr. Frankenstein's laboratory."

There was just too much to absorb in one glance. Harry and I gaped until I finally thought to close the closet door behind us, and then we gaped some more as we ducked into the room and walked the length of it.

I stopped dead in my tracks when I spotted something that clearly wasn't just about business or science.

It was about *us*.

There was a chart rail on one wall, lined with graphs labeled with the Angel kids' names. I think I stopped breathing as I advanced toward the chart bearing my name.

This is what my chart looked like, friend. Along the bottom line, the X-axis, were all the years of my life. Down the left-hand side, the Y-axis, were letters and acronyms that I didn't recognize—XL, Num, SPD, HiQ, Znth, ProMax, and Lazr. A zigzagging trend line tracked unnamed data points from the bottom left to the top right.

"*Harry*," I called out to my twin. He came to my side, and I didn't even need to look at him to register his disbelief. "Malcolm was tracking something about us here. The lines in this chart show some kind of growth or volatility. And tell me what you think of the letters on the Y-axis. It's code. And I don't get it. At all."

My brother wasn't listening to me. He had pulled a chair up to a computer and was tapping at the keyboard, saying, "Oh my *God*, oh my *God*."

I went to Harry and looked over his shoulder.

"Put your nerd brain on this, will you, Tandy? It's the key to the colored lines, and also to those letters. They have to be acronyms for some kind of chemicals."

He had to be right. It came to me in a flash.

"Those chemicals are drugs, Harry. *Our* drugs. These letters stand for the names of our pills. The colors match the colors of our pills. And these data points indicate how we responded to those pills. Gotta be our performance. Our aptitude. Whatever Malcolm was trying to track. God—he was studying us like a family of little rats."

Harry had enlarged his chart on the monitor. "It looks like Malcolm changed my pills all the time," he said. "See?"

I saw what he meant. Where my chart had staggered lines and a rising trend line, the lines on Harry's graph crisscrossed, shot up into peaks, plunged into troughs, and then staggered again.

"He was experimenting with my life," Harry said. "He switched out my pills regularly. I always thought…"

"That they were vitamins," I finished for him. "Maybe steroids for Matty and Hugo."

"He was trying out new formulations," Harry said, pointing out the numbers and combinations of colored lines. "No wonder I'm so emotional. Apparently he just couldn't figure out how to fix me. How to make me right. Like a real Angel."

I wanted to soothe Harry and tell him it wasn't true, but in my gut I knew he was right. "Well, then, Harry, you were a perfect experiment."

"He loved a challenge, didn't he?" Harry shook his head. "He was running experiments on us. And with me...Well, he never did end up fixing me. And now he never will." Harry grunted woefully. "We're doomed, aren't we, Tandy?"

# 57

Harry and I were breathless, panting like marathon runners near the end of the race. We were freaking out—because we were *freaks*.

We'd always known it, but until now, we hadn't known *why* we were so different from everyone else. And now we knew.

*Our parents had been dosing us with pharmaceutical drugs, messing with our minds and bodies our whole lives.*

Harry stayed at the computer, opening files and reviewing them and sending things to his own e-mail address. And then he stopped on one file.

"Tandy, listen to this. Here's a memo from dear old Uncle Peter to dear old Dad."

So Uncle Peter knew about this, too?

" 'Regarding escalating drug protocols and increasing the percentage of SPD for Matthew.' SPD for Matthew. Do you think that stands for *speed*?"

"XL could be *excel*," I said, reading farther down the open page. "It says here that I was taking XL, Znth, Num, ProMax, and Lazr. Maybe Lazr stands for *laser*."

"As in laser focus?"

"Could be, right?" I said.

"What did they *do* to us, Tandy? What did they *do*? 'Are we not Men?' " Harry was quoting one of his favorite writers, H. G. Wells. In his novel *The Island of Doctor Moreau*, animals were changed into humans in a laboratory called the House of Pain—and if the animals didn't obey the laws of the lab, they got really Big Chops.

So the Angel kids are bona fide characters in a science-fiction story? Even though I already had my suspicions about the pills, I felt dizzy with the shock of the truth. I grabbed a countertop to steady myself against the rush.

No, we were not men.

We'd been exploited, used without our knowledge or permission. We were lab rats to Malcolm and Peter, scientific works in progress, and there was no excuse in the world for it, even if they thought the drugs were for our own good.

Harry pulled up Matty's chart and checked the uptick in SPD against the date of Peter's memo. They matched. The drugs had been increased, and the line on Matty's chart rose accordingly. The chart was still open on the computer screen when the door to the lab suddenly opened.

Harry and I both jumped guiltily—we were in Malcolm's private room, and we still had the instinctive fear of a Big Chop.

Hugo stood in the doorway, and he didn't seem very surprised at what he saw. "So," said my little brother, "you guys finally found out Malcolm's secret. It's about time."

# 58

We *didn't have time to question* Hugo about his knowledge of the room until we were in the car. Harry and I agreed that we had to get to Matty right away, so Virgil was driving us to the Meadowlands, the Giants' practice field, an enormous indoor enclosure next to the new stadium. Never mind that it was a Wednesday and that before all this happened, Virgil would have been driving us to school instead. I rubbed my temples with both hands. I couldn't even think about going back to school.

"Hugo, how did you know about Malcolm's secret lab? And why didn't you tell any of us about it? How many times have you been down there?" I was firing off questions as quickly as I thought of them.

"I'd seen Malcolm go in the closet lots of times. One time he forgot to lock the door behind him and I followed. It wasn't hard."

"But why didn't you say anything?" Harry asked.

Hugo just shrugged. "I never went into the lab. I just knew about it. Who cares about a stupid lab? Dad was a scientist, after all."

This sounded suspicious to me, but I wasn't sure how to reframe the question so I could pry some answers out of Hugo. We sat in silence as I thought, Harry brooded, and Hugo amused himself by hanging his head out the window.

When we finally arrived at the field, we quickly headed for where the "Ginats" were working out in full pads— running plays, butting heads. I saw Matthew catch a long pass, after which his coach motioned to him to wrap it up and head to the locker room.

He was trotting off the field as Harry, Hugo, and I ran toward him.

Matthew pulled up short and squinted at us. He had his fighting face on. "What are you guys doing here?"

"We need your help, Matty," I told him firmly.

"Really? You need help from a *killer*?"

"Can you blame me for trying to find out who killed them?"

"What was it that Malcolm used to say? That you're as sensitive as a truck?"

"Sure. I get high praise for my insensitivity."

"Well, that's certainly true." He smiled. And when Matthew Angel smiled, he outshined any movie star you can name. "Look, Tandy. I adore you. You're my sister. But the further I get from the Angel family tree, the fewer nuts will fall on my head."

He turned toward the locker room again, and the three of us went after him like a pack of mutts running after a car.

"Matty, we need your help because…well, it's just like you said in the beginning: One for all and all for one is the best way to proceed now," I said. "The only way. So hear me out."

"Keep me out of it. I have enough problems of my own." He waved us away like we were gnats.

"*Hey.*"

Matthew stopped walking and turned to face me. "You're not going to change my mind."

I put *my* mad face on.

"If you don't help us, we're going to have to go public with what we know. I mean it, Matthew."

"Get serious. I'm not afraid of you, Tandy."

"We know about the pills. We found the charts. We'll

find the formulas, too—I'm sure of it. But even now I can say with confidence that those pills have been behind your success, Matty. Your speed and agility. It's called performance enhancement."

"Really?"

"Really. It's only because drug screens don't catch Malcolm's formulas that you haven't been caught, but now we know. And if we talk, your career is *over*."

Matthew said, "You'd go that far? You'd actually blackmail me? If you go public, all of us will be exposed. You, Hugo, and you, too, Harry. I guess you won't be playing Lincoln Center again."

Harry had been teetering on the brink of a meltdown for days, and at Matthew's words, he finally lost it. He opened his mouth and let out a high C note. And held it. And held it some more.

If a shooting star could make music, it would sound like Harry's high note. The other football players stopped short. Everyone on the field froze and pinned their eyes on my twin.

When Harry finally ran out of air, I said to Matthew, "With your help or without it, we're going to clean up this mess. We're going to do it right now. Are you with us or against us, big brother?"

# 59

*Angel Pharmaceuticals occupies a daunting,* slate-gray, nine-story building on Eleventh Avenue and Forty-eighth Street, in the heart of New York's Hell's Kitchen district.

As we got out of the car, Matthew said to me, "I hope you know what you're doing."

"You have to ask? This is going to be the grand finale, Matty. You can thank me later."

We climbed two flights of metal steps to a landing. I pressed the buzzer on the wall and looked up at the camera mounted above the door. A moment later the door opened, and we entered the building onto a factory floor.

The action on the floor was mesmerizing. The ceiling was at least thirty feet high. On one side of the vast warehouse, ice cream–colored pills poured down chutes and were funneled into bottles that moved along a conveyer belt like little soldiers. The bottles were then stacked into cartons by faceless people in powder-blue masks, caps, and paper gowns.

This mechanized operation, those rivers of pills—just like the ones I'd been taking since I was old enough to hold a sippy cup—gave me the creeps.

"It smells like pills in here," Hugo said. "Gross."

On the other side of the floor, backup alarms sounded as forklift operators drove back and forth with pallets stacked with cartons, wheeling, reversing, and placing the cartons high up on shelves.

The cartons were labeled in Chinese.

And it might not surprise you at this point to learn that I can actually read Chinese.

The shipping address was Beijing, China. And the cartons were labeled with product names: "Strong As Ox Pills"; "Very Smart Children Pills"; and one I had to think about for a moment…and then I had it: "No Worries Pills."

Even if I hadn't been able to read the labels, I could have guessed at the contents of the cartons; I could smell ylang-ylang and viburnum in the air—and a particular fragrance that I thought of as "yellow."

If I was right, the drugs that had been tested on us—
XL, Lazr, SPD, and the others—were soon going to be
dispensed far and wide. Angel Pharma was shipping our
drugs *overseas*.

Had that always been the Angel brothers' plan?

Hugo was taking pictures with his cell phone, and he
didn't care who saw him. He had no inhibitions. He was a
certifiable genius and as strong as a wrestler. What would
he have been like without the pills?

What would *any* of us be like without the pills?

Could I ever be normal?

And the most difficult question: Did I even *want* to be?

# 60

*I led the charge with an electric,* righteous anger that I could feel all the way to the ends of my hair. We piled into the elevator, looked up at the rising numbers without speaking, and then poured out on the executive floor as soon as the doors opened. Even Matty looked determined as we marched directly into the main conference room without knocking.

Uncle Peter sat in a large chair at the head of a long glass table, and he was bent over his laptop. He looked up when we walked in.

"Take your seats," he said. "Try not to smudge the table. What could be so important that it couldn't wait, Tandoori?"

Just looking at my uncle's smug and unpleasant face made my insides smolder. I thought about the memos he'd exchanged with my father, discussing our pills as if we lived in cages and would die in them, too. I waited until Matthew, Harry, and Hugo were all seated. I remained standing, pacing the conference room as I prepared to speak. I made sure to leave the door wide open so everyone nearby would hear what I was about to say.

"We have evidence that you and Malcolm used us as lab animals, that you pumped us full of performance-enhancing drugs."

There was a long silence as Uncle Peter took that in. Then he said, "You're not joking, are you? That's seriously what you think?"

"And then, so that you could own the patents on these drugs and, of course, take over the whole company, you killed our parents."

Uncle Peter cringed. It was just a quick flicker across his features, like a flash of heat lightning. Then his face closed like a fist. He shot up from his chair and slammed his hands down on the table.

"*I* killed Malcolm? You're accusing me of killing my own *brother*?"

"We have pictures of the factory," I said, standing my ground. "We still have pills squirreled away in our apartment for comparison. Our parents' deaths will make you close to a billionaire, Uncle Peter. That means you're the only person with both access to our parents *and* the motive to kill them," I went on, feeling the whole blazing truth setting me free. "If you admit your role in this scheme, if you confess to the killings, we'll give you a chance to go to the police on your own. I think Philippe will be able to cut you a deal. Just *confess*."

# 61

Peter rolled up his shirtsleeves and sat down again in his oversized chair. He wheeled it forward and clasped his hands on the table in front of him. He'd gathered himself during my speech, and his smirk was back, as if it had been riveted to his face.

"This ugly speech you've just given, Tandoori, is entirely speculation, and based on circumstantial evidence at best." There was an angry thrum in his voice, like the lethal sound of a downed power line. The man was scary. "You have a theory based on a hypothesis. No witnesses. No physical evidence. And you expect anyone to believe this utterly libelous fabrication?"

"So you're not denying it?" Matthew asked, clenching his fists.

"I could go into more detail about the memorandums between you and my father," I said, "but we asked our driver to wait. Our next stop, Uncle Peter, is the Twentieth Precinct."

"First of all, you little termites," Peter said, staring at each of us in turn, "the pills aren't drugs. They're natural ingredients, supplements that are manufactured for export and sale outside of the USA. They don't even have to be FDA approved. There's nothing illegal about them, do you understand?"

"You expect us to believe that those pills we took our entire lives are made of rainbow dust and flower petals? Really?" Harry asked. I was proud of him for joining in the fight.

"I'm speaking, Harrison. My turn. Second, your father loved you. I don't know why; it makes no sense to me at all. You're all snots. But then, snottiness runs on your mother's side of the family. The bottom line is that your father would never hurt any of you. You all did very well on rainbow dust and flower petals. I'd say that you excelled, in fact. You're *welcome*, Tandoori. Children."

He nodded at us, still sneering.

"Third, here are the facts. *I* founded Angel Pharmaceuticals. Me. *I* brought your father in as a consulting partner. He owned twenty percent of the firm when he died. That's twenty percent of the debts, too, and right now, we're underwater. So I would have been happy for Malcolm to have bought me out, understand? His death only adds to my problems.

"And last, Tandy, you self-important twerp, eighteen people were having dinner with me when your parents were killed. In my apartment. All eighteen of them swore to the police that I was with them until you called me that night."

"You could have used some kind of time-release formula," I said. "You encapsulated a poison and put it into a bottle of something, and my parents innocently—"

"Get out of here," our uncle said. "All of you."

He looked as if I'd struck him across the face with a whip. And I saw something else, too. There were tears in his eyes. Uncle Peter was actually crying.

"Did you hear what I said?" His voice was shaking.

My brothers stared mutely, but then Hugo, who had been sitting beside me, got up and walked over to Uncle Peter—and tipped his chair back. The wheels shot out from under the chair and Peter went down with a satisfying crash.

"I hate you for turning us into freaks," Hugo said, standing over our uncle. "I hate you with all my heart. Just like I hated them."

Uncle Peter scrambled to his feet and lunged at Hugo, but Matthew swiftly intervened and shoved Peter against the wall and held him there, about a foot off the ground.

*"I'm your guardian!"* our uncle shouted. "I can turn some of you over to the state, understand me? Without me, you three underage ingrates are wards of the state." Uncle Peter had turned bright red, and it occurred to me that he might have a heart attack right there in front of us.

I said, "Matty, let him go. Let him *go*! He didn't kill Malcolm and Maud."

# 62

*How did I know that?* To be honest, I didn't. But he was right. He could turn us over to the state, and despite his obvious hatred for us, the fact of the matter was that he couldn't have been at our apartment when Malcolm and Maud were killed.

"Nice going, Tandy," said Matthew. "You really bit off more than you could chew there."

"You're going to blame me for this?" I fixed him with a steely glare. "You were backing me up the whole time, until he brought out the part about witnesses."

"It doesn't matter," said Harry. "We all heard how Uncle Peter talked about his brother. He loved Malcolm.

He couldn't have killed him any more than we could kill one another. Right?"

"Whatever," Hugo said, punching the air. "Tipping him over was the best part."

As we left Hell's Kitchen in the town car, Virgil looked at us anxiously through the rearview mirror.

"Are you kids okay? We're going to the police station on Eighty-second Street, right?"

"There's been a change of plans, Virgil," I said in a small, raspy voice. "Please take us home."

Since discovering that Uncle Peter and our father had used us as guinea pigs, I had been feeling enough fury to ignite the family business and burn the building down. I leaned back against the dark leather seat as my three brothers talked about what they wanted to do to Uncle Pig.

Matthew was saying, "I can't believe what we just did in there. I think Uncle Pig could get me on assault. Tandy, you could get charged with libel or something like that. And, Hugo. What happened to you, little man?"

"I had to stick up for us. I felt…angry. Violent."

"I've been there," said Matty. "Like, every day of my life."

I was feeling an ache that I didn't recognize. It was as if

there were a radioactive seed inside my chest, growing hotter and more toxic by the minute.

Was I suffering from a guilty conscience? Had the pill called Num protected me from this feeling until now? And what did I feel so guilty about? Uncle Peter had been instrumental in drugging his own family. That was heinous. That was criminal.

But had he committed murder?

I really wasn't so sure. I kept thinking about how he'd flinched when I'd accused him. And I had seen him cry.

Still, I'd accused him publicly. Everyone in his entire office probably heard what I'd said. And if he didn't kill Maud and Malcolm, I'd done him wrong.

I said to my brothers, "Uncle Peter might be Dr. Frankenstein. He might even be a murderer. But I have to account for what I did to him. I have to apologize for that."

"Are you kidding?" Matthew said.

I shook my head. "I have to take back what I said."

Hugo said, "Are you really sorry? Or are you just saying you're sorry because you feel you have to say it? You're supposed to apologize with a true heart. Samantha told me that."

"What do you mean, 'true heart'?" I asked.

Hugo shrugged. Harry laughed. Matthew snorted.

I glared at my brothers. "What?"

"If you have to ask, it kind of defeats the purpose," said Matthew.

"Aw, Tandy, I feel sorry for you." Harry smiled wistfully. "I think getting off the drugs is gonna be great for you."

I sniffed, feeling patronized. But...it was true. In some ways, I was like a child.

And that was going to change, really soon.

I pulled out my phone and googled *apology* and found that a true apology has three components.

One: *I'm sorry.*

Two: *I promise never to do it again.*

Three: *What can I do to make it up to you?*

And four, according to Hugo by way of Samantha, an apology has to be made with a true heart. I guessed that meant I'd need to be sincere.

I didn't really know how to do that. I still hated Uncle Peter for his role in all of this. He'd stepped into our personal business many more times than you even know about.

But I would have to try, because I had been wrong.

And even though my parents were gone, I still felt horrified by the thought that they would be ashamed of me.

*I called Peter.* Here's what I said.

"Uncle Peter, it's Tandy."

Silence.

"I'm sincerely sorry for accusing you of killing my parents. I know you loved Malcolm—"

He hung up on me.

I called him back two more times, and when he didn't answer, I left my full apology on his voice mail. Then I called Sergeant Caputo. In a strange way, I felt like apologizing to him, too. He was driven to the point of being abusive—just like I'd been—but I thought he was trying his best to solve the murders.

"It's Tandoori Angel. I have reason to believe that Peter

Angel is shipping illegal drugs to China. Yes, I'm sending you some photos via e-mail right now. You may want to notify the Drug Enforcement Administration."

After sending the incriminating photos to Caputo, I clicked off my phone and looked out the window as we sped up the West Side Highway.

It was starting to rain. I calmed myself by counting the swipes of the windshield wipers and relaxing into the whooshing sound of our wheels speeding over the wet pavement.

And I had the recurring thought that had been driving me since I found out that Malcolm and Maud were dead.

In fact, I felt it more strongly than ever.

Whoever had killed my parents had been an "inside" person who was certain that he was smart enough to out-wit all of us.

I didn't know if he'd robbed us of our parents or liber-ated us. Either way or both ways, I couldn't let the killer continue to live among us unpunished.

I couldn't let the killer win.

# CONFESSION

*I just need to clarify something.* When I apologized to Uncle Peter, it wasn't the first time I'd ever apologized to someone.

After all, Malcolm and Maud taught us manners. They taught us how to say "I'm sorry" when we accidentally spilled something on their expensive Italian furniture, or when we were rude to our siblings, or when we had offended our elders.

They just never really talked about *how* to realize when you've hurt someone, and then once you realize it, to own up to it, and to tell them you're sorry. With a true heart.

And now that I know about this "true heart" thing, I'm realizing that this isn't the first time I've ever apologized to someone about a really bad thing I did.

I apologized to Harry once, didn't I? It feels like so long ago.

Little bits of a mosaic are floating into my memory, with pieces missing in between them. It's like I can only remember flashes before everything gets whisked away.

I hear Harry crying, "How could you? How could you not tell me about him? About *any* of it? How could you try to escape *without* me? *You left me alone—to be eaten by the tigers!*"

And the worst part: I hear my sweet twin brother screaming at me, "*I hate you!*"

I *had* abandoned him, hadn't I? My dearest brother, my flesh and blood. What was I thinking? I'd been so selfish.

Is this what falling in love does to a person? Does it make you lose all sense? Is that why my parents wanted to shelter me from it?

I hear myself apologizing to Harry, begging for forgiveness: *I'm so sorry, Harry. I don't understand why I left. I deserve to be hated, shunned, punished—with no mercy.*

And I remember the promise I made: *I promise I'll never abandon you, or anyone in this family, again.*

Including Malcolm and Maud.

Which was why I was so bound and determined to find their killer. I owed it to them.

# 64

"*Oh, God,* I can't take this anymore," said Harry. "I really can't take it."

Satellite vans from local and national news outlets lined Central Park West, spilling around the corner and down Seventy-second Street, circling the Dakota like a twenty-first-century wagon train.

"Try to think of it this way," I said to Harry. "We want the same thing as the press. They want to know who did it, and why."

Virgil parked in a no-parking zone, a prohibited space next to a fire hydrant right in front of the building. The rain was coming down even harder than before. High winds were thrashing treetops in the park and gusting up the avenue.

A hundred black umbrellas lifted and riffled in the wind.

"Just look at the buzzards," Hugo said. "I'd like to punch every single one of them in the face."

"That's my baby brother, Hugo," Matty said, and laughed out loud. "Let him out!"

It was astonishing.

All of these reporters were waiting for *us*.

I'd seen pictures of the media frenzy after John Lennon had been shot, murdered by a lunatic at the Dakota. This was what the media circus looked like then. And now there was another juicy story that would not die. A prominent couple had been murdered, and one or all of their kids had likely done it. A quote from any of us, or even from a nosy neighbor, would make headlines and secure the top-of-the-hour news slot.

"Ready to do this, Matthew?" Virgil said.

We all took a deep breath and got out of the car. With Matthew and Virgil parting the crowd, we bumped along in formation, ducking rain and umbrellas as we headed toward the Dakota's front doors.

We were almost there when a woman slammed into me

and said, "Whoops, I'm sorry." It was Kaylee Kerz, a reporter I'd seen on ESPN so many times that I felt as though I knew her. But apart from the "whoops," she didn't notice me. Her eyes were on Matty.

"Matthew! Matthew, could you comment on your suspension from the NFL?"

If it hadn't been so unnerving to be in the thick of such mayhem, I would have laughed out loud at the idea of the NFL suspending my brother. They would *never* do that. He was the icon of all sports icons. He was a superstar.

But when Matthew turned to her, I saw his expression, and he wasn't shocked at what the TV reporter had asked him. He didn't look as though the ground had opened up under him, either. He didn't even look angry.

Matthew almost always looked angry.

"Hi, Kaylee. Nice to see you," he said. "Want to make some news together?"

# 65

*Five minutes later I was sitting* next to Harry in our home theater, watching Matty talking to Kaylee Kerz on the TV.

"I'm well aware of the suspension," Matthew said to her, "but it's bogus. My reputation has been harmed by this illegal action, and my lawyers are drawing up a lawsuit against the NFL as we speak."

"Can you please elaborate, Matthew? I'm sure your fans would like to know what's behind this news, and they'd like to hear it from you, in your own words."

Matthew nodded and said to the reporter, "This isn't really about my words. Every NFL contract contains a clause that states there are certain player infractions that are considered detrimental to the league. So if you attempt to fix a game, get caught with drugs, shoot yourself in the foot with a gun, hold up a bank—anything like that—you can be suspended, maybe indefinitely.

"The commissioner is saying that because I was arrested, I'm 'impairing public confidence' in the league."

"But the charges against you were dropped," said Ms. Kerz.

"Exactly," Matthew said. He seemed to be stroking the reporter with his eyes. "The charge against me was for 'interfering' with the police. But it's false. It never happened. The only place I run interference is on the field, and since I'm a receiver, I don't even do that very often."

The reporter tilted her face up to Matthew and laughed—somewhat flirtatiously, in my opinion. So what else is new?

"But I have a feeling that this suspension has nothing to do with my one night in jail," Matthew continued. "I think it has to do with my personal life. And you know, Kaylee, there's nothing in my contract that says a complicated love life is punishable by suspension."

"Of course not," said Kaylee Kerz.

Other reporters were shouting questions, closing in,

angling microphones and cameras toward my brother as the wet wind blew around him. He didn't flinch.

"Thanks for the opportunity to go on the record," Matty said.

"Matthew, what about the deaths of your parents? What can you tell us?"

"I have no firsthand knowledge and no comment about this tragedy that's happened to my family," he said. He gave the camera a little wave and a thumbs-up before he walked away from the reporter and toward the Dakota's entrance.

Kerz turned back to face the lens.

"That was Matthew Angel, answering our questions about his suspension by the National Football League. He said unequivocally that—"

I clicked off the television and Hugo, Harry, and I stared at one another in disbelief until we heard our front door open.

Matty poked his head around the corner. "How'd I do?"

"Great. Really well done, Matty." I narrowed my eyes at him. "So why didn't you tell us about the suspension?"

Matty shrugged. "You didn't give me a chance. As soon as I saw you, you were practically threatening to tell the

NFL that I was guilty of taking performance-enhancing drugs. You wanted me out anyway, didn't you?"

"Of course not! I—"

"And don't *you* talk to *me* about keeping stuff to myself, Tandy," Matthew growled. "You're guilty of that more than anyone else in this family."

I was silent. *Guilty.* Harry jumped weakly to my defense. "Tandy *selectively discusses*," he offered. "She doesn't *hide*."

"Whatever you want to call it, it proves my point." Matthew chortled. "It's all about spin."

Hugo leapt from his chair and shouted "Hup!" as he went barreling into his hero's arms.

As the two headed for Hugo's room, I thought about Matty's interview.

Everything in Matty's life was going directly down the drain: dead parents, pregnant girlfriend who was saying the baby wasn't his, and tarnish on his sterling reputation that might get him booted out of the big league. Yet, none of that loss and chaos had been evident when he'd spoken with a reporter who could salvage his reputation.

*It's all in the spin.*

Why did that suddenly sound scary to me?

Matthew had not only won Kaylee Kerz over, he'd

represented himself perfectly and then effortlessly deflected her questions about our parents' murders.

The ability to perform flawlessly under pressure was what made Malcolm think that Matty could be president one day.

It was also why he thought Matthew was a sociopath.

*News of the Angel family scandal* was aired on every channel that night.

It's *crazy* to see yourself on television—crazy in a really bad way. You have no control over what people say about you. They can lie viciously, and they do. I'm beginning to have some compassion for Lindsay Lohan and Britney Spears and everybody else caught in the media glare.

Believe me, it's beyond awful.

Three one-hour specials about our family were going to air in the same time slot. *Under Suspicion* was the most outrageous of the shows. The host was Anthony Imbimbo, who was known for his investigative reporting of true-crime stories. That night's special episode was titled

"*Under Suspicion*: The New York Angel Family, Part One."

The piece started with footage of our parents' bodies being roughly unloaded from the ambulance behind the medical examiner's office at dawn. Then Imbimbo narrated the fast-forward version of our parents' lives in tiny bio snippets. Malcolm and Maud were portrayed as cold-hearted capitalists without any humanity.

"The Angel family is no stranger to scandal, dating back to the Angel dynasty's patriarch, William Harrison Angel, who, as a result of his spectacular gambling habit, lost more than half of the giant fortune he acquired by investing in Manhattan real estate. Still, the family managed to hold on to their magnificent wealth, and to increase it by many millions over the next several generations. In fact, for nearly a century, an often-mocked urban legend has circulated in elite Manhattan society about an *actual* Angel family guardian angel, supernaturally bound by God—or perhaps the devil—to ensure that the family is protected from any trouble it makes. And trouble, it seems, has a habit of seeking out the Angels."

I rolled my eyes, amazed that such a silly story had found a way to live on into the twenty-first century. Despite how many still believe in the American dream, people never seem to grasp that our wealth has come from hard work. They have to make up stories that explain it away.

On TV, Imbimbo continued on with his blather. But I wasn't able to dismiss the next part quite so easily.

"When the family's eldest daughter, Katherine, died in a motorcycle crash in South Africa, her death was ruled suspicious at first."

I stood up, not sure I really wanted to have this wound reopened.

"But the case was closed less than forty-eight hours later."

I started punching buttons on the remote.

"And the most recent case was the quickly squashed scandal involving the disappearance of the Angels' other teenage daughter, Tandoori, known as 'Tandy' to the few who have regularly interacted with this very sheltered child. Just a year ago, the girl was found—"

I clicked the power button on the remote.

But not before setting the DVR.

Someday, I might be ready to watch that part.

# CONFESSION

*I clicked off the TV just* in time. Those four words were enough. Too much.

*The girl was found.*

Had I been lost?

Malcolm and Maud would have told the police that I was lost, I'm sure. But something told me I wasn't. My mind was starting to feel like it was emerging from a fog, allowing me to trust something beyond the facts stored in my conscious mind. It was starting to allow me to trust my gut.

And this is the truth my gut told me.

I'd been found, but I hadn't been lost, and I hadn't been alone.

I closed my eyes and lay down on the couch. I saw the ghostly face in my mind again, and this time I wasn't scared of it. This time I didn't pass out. I concentrated on it.

His face wasn't clear enough yet, and I couldn't tell how old he was. But I could remember now how desperately I had wanted to be with him. Passionately, you might even say. I think I would have done anything for him to help me get out of the prison. The prison that was my life.

We were escaping.

He had promised me freedom. And I'd tasted it—I could almost taste it now. I had flashes of his fingers interlacing with mine. Leaving under cover of dark. Looking at the stars together. Spooning together in the backseat of his car. Laughing as he tried to educate me about all the pop music on his iPod, and then enjoying long, peaceful stretches of classical music when I switched over to satellite radio. We even started compiling a sound track for our getaway.

It seemed so easy. So perfect.

We were headed for Canada, and we got as far as a McDonald's in northern New York State, where we stopped for breakfast at dawn, snuggling into the same side of a booth. I'd never been to a McDonald's in my life. I remember being happy at the thought of how enraged Malcolm would be to see me there, and thinking I had the whole world—the *real* world—ahead of me.

Until the place was stormed by bunch of thugs.

I had made two mistakes: not being a hundred percent aware

of my surroundings at all times, like I usually was, and seating myself on the outside edge of the booth. So that when they came for me, I was easily yanked out.

In my mind's eye, I can't see his face as I was being torn away from him forever. But I can feel his arm around my waist and his hand clutching at my sweater to hold me to him. I can hear his voice shouting: *Tandy, they can't do this. They can't keep you away from me. They can't keep you in a cage. Don't let them.*

And his last words: *I'll come back for you.*

But he never did.

My last sight of him was a view of his hunched-over back as he was shoved into an Escalade. And as I screamed his name and tried to fight off my captors, I saw who was supervising the whole operation from just a few paces away: *Uncle Peter.*

That's when I realized Malcolm and Maud had been tracking me.

Like a dog with a chip, penned in by an electric fence.

# 67

*I sat there in the theater* for a few minutes, taking deep breaths in through my nose, and then exhaling through my mouth. Some of Dr. Keyes's techniques still worked wonders for me. Soon I mustered up the courage to switch on the TV show in progress, leaving the recorded DVR segment for later. Much, much later.

I heaved a sigh of relief. I'd rejoined at a commercial break. When the show returned to the air, I saw the four of us wading into the dense field of black umbrellas as we went into the Dakota.

Then the show cut to a close-up of Matthew talking to Kaylee Kerz, lifting his shades to fasten his blue eyes on her, then giving a thumbs-up to the camera. Matty looked slick. Too slick.

The show cut again, to Tony Imbimbo interviewing Capricorn Caputo.

Caputo hacked a couple of times into his hand then said darkly, "It's an ongoing investigation. I can only say that we have suspects and we're confident that we will bring the killer to justice."

Cut again to Imbimbo, stopping neighbors on their way into the Dakota. Mrs. Hauser, wearing gold lamé and a hat, complained to the TV shark, "We're now looking into taking legal action against the Angels. This kind of disturbance is against the rules."

I blurted out, "Legal action? What kind of legal action? They wouldn't try to *evict* us, would they?"

Then documentary filmmaker Nathan Beale Crosby, wearing his trademark red baseball hat and matching glasses, rushed past, almost knocking Mrs. Hauser down. Crosby wouldn't stop for someone else's camera.

But Morris Sampson happily stepped up to Imbimbo's microphone.

Imbimbo introduced Sampson as a number one bestselling author, which made me snicker. "Bestselling where? Timbuktu?"

Sampson said to Imbimbo, "I've heard *privately* that Maud and Malcolm Angel were *poisoned* by a toxin that even the city's forensic lab can't identify. You know, of course, that the family manufactures pharmaceutical drugs."

Imbimbo could hardly hold back his elation at the implied connection between Angel Pharmaceuticals and the poison that killed my parents.

I felt as though I'd been shot between the eyes.

"Mr. Sampson, who do *you* think killed the Angels?"

"I'm not going to point any fingers," Sampson said. "But if I were writing this story as a novel—and let me emphasize the words *work of fiction*—I would say that all four children are smart and crafty enough to commit murder. The four of them, working in concert, could probably get away with it."

Sampson's remark signaled the end of the program.

The show's signature close was a series of full-screen photos accompanied by the sound of a camera flash as each picture filled the screen and the words *Under Suspicion* were stamped across each image.

Matthew, flash-*bam*.

Me, flash-*bam*.

Harry, flash-*bam*.

Hugo, flash-*bam*.

*Bam, bam, bam, bam.*

"Under suspicion of committing murder by the NYPD."

What was even worse—much worse—was that I had the exact same list of suspects.

# 68

I'd told Hugo and Harry that we were going to return to school on day seven. At the time, of course, I hadn't known that our dirty laundry was going to be aired on national television the night before.

And so that morning, I was paralyzed. I couldn't get out of bed. Embarrassment was an emotion I'd been shielded from for most of my life, either by the mood-altering drugs or simply by being sheltered from my peers. Now, humiliation was crippling me.

*Don't let this crush you, Tandy*, the little voice inside said. *You're stronger than this. And you're much stronger than those drugs ever were. Trust yourself.*

And that's what I did. I roused my brothers and forced

myself out the door with my chin up, convinced that academics would be just what I needed to reestablish some normalcy and balance in my life.

All Saints is kind of like an old-fashioned one-room schoolhouse—except that it's not. All Saints is a privately owned, Gothic-style, former Lutheran church on the Upper West Side of Manhattan. Malcolm and Maud loved this school for its small and exclusive enrollment, and because Headmaster Timothy Thibodaux is unfailingly demanding and uncompromising. The law of order is maintained there, and Harry and I had front-row seats because of our consistently high grade point averages.

But as Harry, Hugo, and I entered the school, I wondered for the first time if our top grades were due to our hard work or simply the result of Malcolm's jelly bean–colored pills.

What kind of mind did I have *without* them?

I had to know.

I was hoping for a rigorous academic workout that morning. I wanted to be pushed and pressured so much that I couldn't think about anything else.

We turned right off the narthex and climbed the familiar stairway. Our classroom was there, under the soaring cathedral ceiling, with a view of the altar and the nave that had been turned into a gallery for the works and awards of all the kids who'd ever graduated from All Saints.

Mr. Thibodaux was waiting for us at the top of the stairs. His hands were clasped in front of him, and his snappy jacket and trousers—in autumn bronze and green tones—were as crisp and pressed as if they'd been put together by a celebrity stylist.

Mr. Thibodaux is a smart man, generous with his praise and crystal clear in his criticism. He is exactly the kind of teacher compulsive overachievers like the Angels appreciate. I can usually find the twinkle in his bespectacled blue eyes, but I saw none of that the morning we returned to school. *Mr. Thibodaux must be worried about us*, I thought.

I smiled up into his scowling face. "It's *really* good to be here, Mr. Thibodaux."

"Not for us, Ms. Angel. You didn't get my messages? You've been suspended—all three of you," he said sternly. "And I'm afraid you're going to have to leave these premises right now."

## 69

*I had looked up to Mr. Thibodaux* since I was four years old. I immediately felt the sting of his rejection, but I honestly didn't understand what he had just said to me.

I said stupidly, "I beg your pardon?"

"You can't kick us out!" Hugo said, balling his fists.

Harry looked like he'd been slapped.

"This decision isn't open to discussion, children," Mr. Thibodaux snapped. "You are suspects in the murders of your parents. We wish you the best, of course, but you cannot be here. It would be far too much of a distraction for the rest of the students and staff."

"But the police haven't charged us with murder."

"This is a private school. This whole media circus

is not only disruptive; it could seriously taint our reputation—"

Mr. Thibodaux broke off in mid-sentence as Harry stepped up to him, his jaw thrust forward.

Harry spoke in a hardened tone I hadn't heard from him before. "We're not guilty of anything, sir," he said. "You can't speak to us that way."

Mr. Thibodaux looked surprised. "You're out of line, Mr. Angel."

"*We're* out of line?" Harry said. "All Saints has been paid for our attendance for the full term, sir. We have every right to be here."

One of our classmates, Gabrielle Harvey, was sitting close enough that I could see her roll her eyes dramatically toward another student, Colin Baxter, who was approaching Harry from behind.

I yelled, "Harry, watch out!"

Colin slowly cocked his fist, and Harry spun around just as Colin let his punch fly, hitting Harry square on the jaw. Harry went down, and Colin stood over him, shouting, "Get out of here, you crybaby creep! Get out of our school, mother killer!"

That's when Hugo stepped in.

He growled, lowered his head, and butted Colin Baxter right in the belly. Colin sucked at the air and went down hard. He couldn't catch his breath, and I thought maybe his gut had ruptured.

And that's when things got extremely out of hand.

As Colin got his wind back, he began to wail—which resulted in a bunch of kids screaming for no reason, like they thought someone had just pulled out a lethal weapon or something.

In a sense, I guess we *had*: Hugo.

As Harry struggled to his feet Hugo ran whooping around the loft as though he'd just scored a touchdown at the Meadowlands.

"Everyone, please *stop*!" Mr. Thibodaux yelled.

But no one did.

I had never loved my brothers more.

Mr. Thibodaux was digging in his breast pocket for his phone. "Make no mistake—you *will* be charged with assault!" he shouted at Hugo.

"We're cutting class today," I said to our formerly esteemed headmaster. "Thank you for your help and your concern, Mr. Thibodaux. It's been a comfort to us in our time of need."

# 70

Harry *went straight to his studio* at Lincoln Center to burn off some steam, but Hugo walked home with me. As we passed a corner bodega, he stopped in his tracks.

"Hey, Tandy," he said. "Let's do something crazy."

"What?" I asked, baffled. I was more than a little worried about all of Hugo's newfound anger and how he was planning to channel it.

"Come in here," he said, dragging me into the bodega. "Let's get something we were never allowed to eat at home."

And that's how we ended up back at the Dakota, eating a box of instant macaroni and cheese for lunch at about 10:30 AM.

"This is vile," I commented, reading the ingredients on the package. "I have to agree with Malcolm and Maud on this one. Like they always said, 'You are what you eat....' "

So, what was I, then? What were my brothers? What was my sister Katherine before she was run down in Africa? What were the ingredients in our father's pills?

Not knowing what I'd been swallowing every night for the whole of my life made me question every single thing about myself, down to the size of my feet and the length of my eyelashes.

"So what do we do now?" Hugo asked me.

"Want to help me with my investigation?" I asked him in response.

I didn't have to ask twice.

I grasped the key to my father's home laboratory, which I'd hung from a cord around my neck, and slid it back and forth. I planned to keep the key with me until I had searched Malcolm's lab and computer and found out precisely what the pills were made of and what their side effects were.

I opened the laboratory door and hit the lights. Hugo scooted past me, opened a small refrigerator, and took out a bottle of lemonade. I figured he'd been spying on Malcolm for so long that he knew where everything was in this place.

"What did Matthew tell you about this operation?" I asked Hugo.

"Don't make me snitch on Matty," Hugo said. "Anyway, it doesn't matter. Whatever they are, whatever they do, I *like* my pills. I'm going to keep taking them. I don't want to change. I like myself the way I am."

I had to laugh. I liked him, too.

"We don't know what the long-term effects are," I said, moving toward the computer.

"The short-term effects are that I whooped Colin Baxter's butt. He's not going to mess with any of us ever again."

"Either that or the next time he runs into you, he'll be armed."

"Oh," Hugo said. "Good point."

The computer was still on and its documents still open, just as Harry had left it. I went directly to the memo file and skimmed many years' worth of the back-and-forth exchange between Peter and Malcolm.

One e-mail from Peter to Malcolm read: "Tried adding four RepX on 4/13. No sign of side effects. Will keep an eye out and increase three Genner2.0 to force results."

Malcolm's response read: "Agreed. May decrease focus to increase Genner2.0, but can compensate with one Plav."

It was chilling to read how casually these "supplements"

were discussed. My siblings and I were mentioned, but the memos weren't explicit enough to tell me what I really wanted to know. After another two hours of document review, the question remained: What exactly were our pills made of, and what had they done to us? Could it be reversed?

And if so, was that what I wanted to happen?

Being a "normal" girl had only gotten me into trouble before. Was I ready to try it again now that Malcolm and Maud were out of the picture? I trembled at the memory that was itching to be recognized, relived. My failed attempt at normalcy.

One investigation of mine might be hitting a wall, I thought, but I knew exactly where I had to go to start confronting the mystery of my own history.

I left the lab with Hugo in tow and shut the door behind us.

"Hugo, I think I need to be alone for a little while now," I told him. "Are you okay hanging out by yourself?"

"Sure," Hugo said. "Are *you* ... okay?"

I smiled. "Fine, Hugo. In fact, I think I'm about to have a breakthrough."

And I knew exactly where to start: that file in the cabinet I'd stumbled on earlier while searching Samantha's room. The one labeled J.R.

It was time to get real.

# 71

*I would be lying to you* if I didn't say that it was very, very hard to go back to that filing cabinet, where I knew there could be reams of documents detailing things I wasn't ready to face.

So once I had the folder marked J.R. open, I took my time. Slowly, slowly, I leafed through the thick stack of pages of my own calligraphic replica of the poem "Maud," one of several Big Chops I'd had to do after I ran away.

I forced myself to read every word of the tortured, dense Victorian poem all over again. A delaying tactic. How much did I want to find what else Maud might have tucked into this folder?

I could delay no further when a newspaper clipping fell

out. Before I could read the headline, I saw a face in the accompanying photo.

Now it was no longer a hazy face in my memory, struggling to come into focus. It was plain as day, the handsome face of the young man I'd run away with. Dark blond, longish, straight hair—and the smile that had in an instant taken me in. Won me over. Made me believe in him. In fact, it had been the only thing I believed in, for that short period of time: that he would save me. That we could save each other.

There it was, in black-and-white. He was a real person. He was beautiful, yet frightening to me somehow. And he was missing.

SON OF STORIED FINANCIER, 18, DISAPPEARS UNDER MYSTERIOUS CIRCUMSTANCES.

My hands were shaking so hard they crumpled the paper. Or maybe I was crumpling it up on purpose. I didn't want to read any more.

*Buck up, Tandy. Read it.*

I took a deep breath, opened the clipping, and got only as far as the first two words:

James Rampling.

# 72

*I'm going to apologize to you,* friend—with a true heart. I'm getting better at that, aren't I?

I just want to say that I'm sorry if I've been confusing you. I don't mean to; it's just that I'm confused myself. And if I could ask a favor, please? I need you to help me understand my own story, even if it takes a little time. Or a long time.

Okay. Now that I know you're on my side, I think I can go on.

I uncrumpled the paper and smoothed it out over and over again, almost as if I were stroking the mysterious face of James Rampling, hoping it would tell me something.

For countless minutes, I didn't even read the article. I just felt myself fall deeper and deeper into those eyes.

Slowly, hypnotically, they took me back to the night of the party.

# CONFESSION

*I didn't go to normal teenage parties*—just adult events, or parties where their kids happened to be around. I stopped getting invited to *real* parties some time ago. But a while back, I heard about a no-adults party a senior was throwing in celebration of his early-admission acceptance to Harvard. It was a silly reason for a party as far as I was concerned, but I decided that I was going to try to go to it. And enjoy it.

Almost as if it were an experiment, or a test.

You see, at school I'd been learning about freedom movements all around the world, from the American Revolution to the Arab Spring, and I'd been thinking a lot about the benevolent dictatorship in which I was being raised. I'd been questioning how benevolent it was. And I was pretty sure I wanted out. At least, that night I was sure.

I saw all the other kids at the party drinking whatever they could find, and in order for this to be a true experiment, I had to do what they did. So I drank, first with caution, then with abandon. I don't even know what it was. Given that I was already under the influence of Malcolm's special cocktail of pills, who knows how it all might have interacted.

It was in the most mundane of places that I met James: standing by a keg. He appeared to be staring at my chest, which didn't exactly make me comfortable.

"Sorry," he said with an embarrassed smile, once he realized what he was doing. "Really. I swear. I was just noticing your necklace." Before I could reply with a skeptical comment, he proved himself honorable. "From Tibet, right? Have you been there?"

"Bhutan, actually," I said, stunned to be meeting a guy who knew even the first thing about Southeast Asian art. My interest was immediately piqued.

"It looks like a *zhi* stone," he went on. "My mother started collecting them when we first went to Tibet. Did you know it's supposed to have protective powers?"

"Of course." I laughed. "It was a gift from my parents."

His eyes flashed a little mischievously. "Who needs a *zhi* stone when you have the legendary Angel guardian angel?"

And so from the very beginning, James Rampling seemed to uncannily know just about everything about me, and to love everything I loved. Within a few minutes we found ourselves talking about the Arab Spring, and then Southeast Asian politics. This continued for at least an hour. By then we'd moved away from the crowd and were sitting halfway up a flight of stairs.

He leaned in closer and gently pushed the hair out of my eyes. "Tandy Angel," he said, in an almost reverential, hushed way. "Where have the tigers been keeping you?"

"In a cage," I said. "What do you think?"

"What do I think?" He stroked my hair again, pushing it behind my ears so he could look straight into my eyes. I instinctively tried to look away, but he took my chin and turned my face back toward his. He wouldn't let me look away.

"I think," he said, "that you need to be let out. The world needs you. I think that you're exquisitely beautiful...and exquisitely smart....And you shouldn't be hidden away in a cage."

As I worked through the memory, I replayed that incredible moment in my mind several times. It was the first time I'd been touched by a boy. And not only were his hands touching my face, but his eyes were touching me, too.

A part of me that had never been touched before.

His eyes lit up suddenly. "The caged bird's 'wings are clipped and his feet are tied,'" he began reciting, not letting his eyes stray from mine. "'So...'"

"'So he opens his throat to sing,'" I finished, staggered by James Rampling once again. He was quoting from my favorite poem at the time, "I Know Why the Caged Bird Sings," by Maya Angelou. It was a poem that seemed to reflect how I felt about my life up to that point. I was surprised that James even knew it.

All the more reason why what happened next seemed like pure magic. As I jumped on the next line, he joined in.

And then we recited the whole poem. Together.

Would you laugh at me, friend, if I said it almost felt like we were reciting wedding vows right there, in the middle of the party? Can you blame me for believing I'd just met the one person in the world I was meant to be with? Who was meant to save me?

The rest of the world had fallen away by that point. James leaned in closer, ran his fingers down the cord that held the pendant around my neck, and let his fingers slowly caress the zhi stone—my "protection"—lying against my chest.

I reached up and rested my hand on his.

The sensation of that connection was almost too intense for my system to handle. I sucked in my breath as I saw him come even closer to my face.

And that's when laws of physics stopped working. Time slowed down as his lips touched mine, so very, very sweetly.

That's where the memory ended. I hit replay.

It was real. The kiss I'd written about had been real. This time, though, I could *feel* it, in every bone in my body.

Replay.

Replay.

Replay.

Each time, I hoped the memory would go a little bit further. I know it went further. Much further. Beyond one kiss. Beyond one night at a party. Beyond a mere fantasy of being touched, embraced, adored by a boy who actually understood me.

Something told me Dr. Florence Keyes had stolen almost every other memory I'd had of James Rampling. And someday, I was going to make her give them all back to me.

But right now, I had this one. I was going to enjoy it, savor it, this rare electric moment when my life had felt real and simple and joyous and free.

Reading the rest of that article could wait. Indefinitely.

# 73

*I put the folder away.* I had made real progress on one front. Now I was going to have to take the bull by the horns to make some headway in my primary investigation: my parents' murders.

I called Matty, Harry, Hugo, Samantha, and Philippe together for another family meeting. We gathered in the study, where my parents had worked every day when they were alive. It was eerie to see Philippe Montaigne behind my father's desk.

I took my mother's chair, and my three brothers and Samantha took seats around the room.

"First things first," I said to Philippe. "No offense, but seriously—are you *our* lawyer? Or do you work for Uncle Peter?"

"I work for the Malcolm Angel family—that is, all of you. And I'm your lawyer, too, Samantha."

"Even though I'm moving out of here tomorrow?"

"You're still my client. I also work for Peter, but I cannot and will not represent anyone besides the four Angel kids if there is a conflict of interest."

"Thank you, Phil," I said. "And if I understand correctly, everything that is said in this room will remain confidential?"

"Absolutely."

"Okay. Now that we're officially lawyered up, let's get started," I said.

I ran the first part of the meeting as if I were a particularly hard-edged prosecutor. I accused everyone of murdering our parents, asking them tough questions and not giving them time to think or lie. They might hate me for what I was doing, but there was no other way. In the end, everyone stuck to their original story. Stuck hard. And I found no holes. Not one.

So I said, "Let's do a secret ballot and see where we stand."

I ripped out a sheet of note paper and passed around the pieces, saying, "Write down who you think killed Malcolm and Maud."

It was very quiet in the room as names were scribbled

down and papers were returned to me. I shuffled the ballots, hoping for a breakthrough of some kind.

Then I read the ballots out loud, one at a time.

"Uncle Peter?"

"Peter."

"Uncle Piggy."

"Uncle P. But maybe not."

"I don't know."

That last one was mine. Everyone at least suspected that Peter had or could have killed our parents. But why weren't the police investigating Peter if it seemed so obvious to us?

"And he's living right here," said Matthew. "Who says he won't kill again? I'm bunking with Hugo indefinitely. Okay, little bro?"

"Are you kidding?" Hugo said. "I'd *pay* you to do that."

Just then, Philippe answered a phone call—and life as we knew it took another nosebleed nosedive.

"Turn on the TV," he snapped.

*The TV reporter Anthony Imbimbo's face* appeared on our fifty-two-inch screen, and he had breaking news for all the world to hear.

"*Under Suspicion* has just learned that actress Tamara Gee is dead. Arthur Boffardi, doorman and superintendent of the building where Ms. Gee has lived for the past three years, found the body just one hour ago. Mr. Boffard—"

"Artie."

"Artie. Can you please tell us what happened?"

I whipped around to look at Matthew, but he was stalking out of the room. At the same time, I heard the intercom buzzer blaring. I ran to catch up with Matty, but he opened the door before I reached him.

He never got out the door.

Sergeant Caputo advanced on Matthew, backing him up as he said, "Matthew Angel, you're under arrest. Put your hands behind your back."

"No *way*," Matthew shouted, "I did *nothing*. I did nothing wrong!"

"Put your hands behind your back."

Three police officers had gathered in our foyer behind Caputo, and it looked like all hell was about to break loose. Matthew's eyes were blazing, and his fists were clenched in front of him. He wasn't going without a fight, and I knew that would only make things worse.

Matthew's scientifically enhanced muscles bulged and rippled under his shirt. The Giants' number one son was going Hulk, right then and there. And nothing could stop him. He bellowed, "*Go ahead. Make me put my hands behind my back.*"

Hayes and Caputo drew their guns. These were real guns, with real bullets, and it occurred to me that cops only draw when they're prepared to shoot somebody.

Caputo shouted in a no-bull way: "Turn and face the wall. Do it *now*."

Matty tightened his fists and swung his head from side to side, as if he were looking for an opening in the defense line. Gun muzzles leveled at his chest. I could hear the gunshots in my head. "Matthew," I whispered, "be smart."

He stopped, turned slowly, and put his hands behind his back. He looked as though he might cry.

Detective Hayes cuffed Matty's wrists and said, "Matthew Angel, you're under arrest for the murder of Tamara Gee. You have the right to remain silent—"

"My lawyer is on the way," Matty said in an unusually subdued voice.

"He can meet you at the Twentieth Precinct."

"My client means I'm right *here*," I heard Philippe say.

I stood frozen with my hands over my mouth as Philippe came around the corner into the foyer. I've never seen Phil lose his temper, but at that moment he looked like a twister about to touch down.

"What are you doing?" he asked Caputo. "What do you *think* you're doing?"

"Angel here is under arrest," said Caputo. "His pregnant girlfriend was killed yesterday. Need I say more?"

"I didn't see her yesterday," Matty blurted out. "I didn't even talk to her. I called her, but she didn't answer."

"Don't say anything, Matthew," Philippe warned him.

"Phil. Ask the kids. I was with them all day yesterday. We went to Pharma together."

"Matthew, I'll meet with you privately, and you can tell me everything."

Matthew said, "But this is a setup. I'm being framed."

Caputo actually laughed as he turned to Hayes, saying, "Golly. I've never heard that one before."

Matty continued to detail where he'd been over the last twenty-four hours: at Angel Pharma, then interviewed by ESPN, and then at home for dinner with us. I was nodding emphatically to corroborate everything he was saying, until my jaw dropped when he added something new.

"After the kids went to bed, I went out to play poker with three of my teammates. They'll tell you. I'll give you their names."

Really? Had Matty gone out while we were all asleep?

"Listen to your lawyer," Hayes said, patting Matty on the shoulder. "Let's go."

Phil said, "I'm coming with my client."

Phil got his own coat out of the hall closet, as well as one for Matty, which he draped over my older brother's shoulders.

I stood under the UFO chandelier as the front door slammed. When Harry and Hugo put their arms around me, I was still standing there like a block of stone, looking at the door.

Just when I was starting to think that our dysfunctional little family was making some progress, my big brother once again became the number one suspect.

# 75

*I was sleeping next to Hugo* when a loud crack sounded in the dark of night. We both shot up out of bed, and Hugo clutched my arm.

"Tandy. *Was that a gun?*"

"Give me your phone," I said.

"It's in the study, I think."

"Mine's there, too. Stay here," I said. "Stay. Right. Here."

"Okay."

Hugo scrambled out from under the covers and grabbed onto a fold of my pajama top.

I hissed, "Stay *here*."

"Okay," he said again. He was still hanging on to me as I moved toward the doorway.

"It's probably Samantha," I said. "She probably just came home."

"Came home and fired a gun?"

"It wasn't a gun," I said, feeling my way in the dark.

The sound had been sharp, like lightning striking a tree or something really heavy dropping to the floor. Like maybe an iron. But who in this house would be using an iron?

Hugo whispered, "Samantha always stops in to see me when she comes home."

I opened Hugo's door just a hair.

"Look," Hugo said, breathing loudly.

He pointed to a thin line of light coming from under the laboratory door. I gripped the key hanging from the chain around my neck. The laboratory door locked automatically when it was closed, and I thought I had the only key.

Clearly, I was wrong. So who had gotten inside Malcolm's lab?

My thoughts were scattered, my focus gone. I had gone too long without a full night of sleep. I found myself thinking that there was an intruder in the house. Only it might be worse than an intruder. It just might be the killer.

The sound we'd heard had been the lab door slamming, hadn't it?

I had to get to a phone and call, of all people, the police.

I was sneaking past the lab with Hugo when the door opened and the light coming from the lab showed the intruder in silhouette. He was a man I knew almost better than I knew anyone.

I screamed, *"Father!"*

*The silhouette looked like my father's*—I swear it did.

But when the man said my name, I realized that the dark—and my fear—had tricked me.

The man in our hallway was my father's only brother, Peter, and the expression on his face told me that he was as freaked out as we were. I could make out the shadow of another figure behind Uncle Peter, which disturbed and disoriented me more. Who would he be bringing into our home at this time of night?

He said, "Hugo. Tandy. Everything is okay. Everything is fine. It's almost three in the morning. Go back to bed."

Uncle Peter was holding a laptop that looked like the one Harry and I had tapped into the day before, the one with the memos about drug protocols that had passed between the Angel brothers. We'd hardly begun our real investigation of those files, and now Uncle Peter was taking away the data that could tell us the formulation and purpose of each of the drugs. There could even be information on that computer that would expose the killer's identity. Had Uncle Peter belatedly realized that it held evidence that would prove that *he* had murdered our parents?

He spoke over his shoulder to the man standing behind him. "Wolfe. Let's go. We're done here."

"Hey!" I shouted. I reached out and switched on the hall lights. "What are you doing, exactly?"

I got a good look at Wolfe. He was gray-haired, with tattoos winding around his neck. He was carrying two boxes of files. I thought I'd seen him driving a forklift at Angel Pharma. "You heard Mr. Angel," he yelled. "Get out of the way, little girl!"

"This is nothing you need to worry about, Tandoori. It's all company property, and Angel Pharma is mine. Just do what I tell you. Both of you, go to your rooms. Now!"

I don't know exactly what set Hugo off, but he went back across the hall—and returned from his room carrying a baseball bat.

He didn't give any warning; he just swung the bat at Wolfe's shins. The man hollered and dropped the file boxes. Then he rolled around on the floor, moaning in pain. Papers were scattered everywhere.

"Damn you, Hugo," Peter spat. "You little SOB!"

"You need to get Mr. Wolfe to the hospital," I said, sounding very cool, even though I was *this close* to running out the door screaming. "I'll take that computer."

"The hell you will."

Hugo assumed a determined batter's stance and held the bat angled fiercely over his shoulder. "I'd give her the laptop, Uncle Peter. If I were you. If I wanted to *walk* out of here."

Uncle Peter seemed paralyzed, no doubt distracted by Wolfe, who was still howling in pain. I took advantage of his moment of confusion and yanked the computer out of his hands, then jumped back out of arm's reach.

My uncle gave me a look that could kill. But he didn't move toward me. He'd been shut down by a ten-year-old.

"There's nothing on that computer that will mean anything to anyone but me. I need your father's records."

"You can have them when I'm done."

"Fine. Knock yourself out, Tandy."

"Thank you. I will."

Uncle Peter pulled out his phone and punched a few buttons. "We need an ambulance," he said, sounding more disgusted than worried. "There's been an accident."

I pulled Hugo into his bedroom and locked us inside. Uncle Peter knocked and said, "Tandy, just give me the computer. It's my property."

I said nothing.

"Go to *hell*!" my uncle shouted through the door.

"You first!" Hugo shouted back. "Take the express train."

"And, Hugo, you'll be going to juvie for this latest transgression. You're an animal."

Hugo and I huddled together as the paramedics came and went. Then, finally, the apartment was quiet again.

Hugo had his bat under the covers with him.

"We aren't safe here," he said. "We aren't safe anywhere, are we?"

*I waited for Hugo to fall asleep,* then slipped out of bed and got busy prowling through the files on the computer—work that was grueling, boring, and maybe even pointless.

The data was all highly technical. There were symbols instead of words. Chains of symbols instead of paragraphs. What text I could interpret was just as Uncle Peter had said—all very specific to the work of Angel Pharma.

I spent an hour opening folders before I came to a file marked "Prometheus."

I got a strong and heady feeling that I'd just found the right door. Maybe? Was it okay to hope? Please?

The Greek myth of Prometheus had been Malcolm's favorite. From the time we were toddlers he'd told us the story about the Titan, a champion of mankind, a wily guy who outwitted the greatest god, Zeus. Prometheus had stolen fire and given it to mortals. That ticked Zeus off, so he gave Prometheus a major Big Chop: Prometheus was chained to a rock, and every day his liver was eaten by an eagle…only to grow back at night…and then get eaten all over again the next day. Try to imagine *that*.

In light of what I'd learned, I wondered if my father saw himself as Prometheus, the giver of gifts to humanity through his mysterious pills.

I opened the Prometheus folder and found hundreds of documents that I could actually read—and mostly understand. This was the treasure trove of information I'd been looking for. I skimmed and absorbed and comprehended charts and lab notes and monographs describing the pills.

Uncle Peter had told me that the pills were largely made of natural ingredients. And that was true.

*Mostly* true.

And also—it was a gigantic lie.

Take this formula, from page 631, for instance: Harry's red sleeping pill contained St. John's wort and passionflower, potent apothecary herbs that promoted healthy sleep and balanced moods and also made pretty decent antidepressants. But there was another ingredient in that compound—AP-T1-4—that I didn't know and was unable to find on the Internet.

What *was* it? What did it *do*? What kind of side effects could Harry be having from it?

My blue pills were called HiQ. They contained natural ingredients that enhanced brain function, including uridine 5'-monophosphate, a nucleotide that stimulates neurons in the brain. But along with the list of natural ingredients and fillers, I found another mystery component: AP-33a.

My yellow capsule was called Lazr. Lazr was made of bacopa monnieri, a plant extract that improves memory and motor learning. Like the other pills, Lazr also contained an unknown additive: AP-101.

According to my growth chart, I'd been taking Lazr since I was one year old. Fifteen years!

What was AP-101? *AP* had to stand for *Angel Pharmaceuticals*. But I found no mention of any of the mystery ingredients in any other Angel Pharma materials or on their websites.

The next file I opened looked like a log of some kind. Each notation had a date and time, followed by descriptive notes about my brothers and me. One from just a few weeks earlier caught my eye: "Tandy showing increased levels of concentration thanks to extra dosage of HiQ, e.g., reading for six hours with no distractions or movement other than turning pages."

How could my father have known I was reading for six hours straight without moving? I remember the novel well; it was one I'd self-selected, for once, because he and Maud were out that day. But if they were out, how did he know what I was doing? Who spied on me for him? I already knew that Uncle Peter was wrapped up in all this, and Samantha had been keeping secrets with my mother for years. Could it be possible one of them was also *watching* us for our parents?

I closed the Prometheus folder and thought about my father as a tireless Titan, developing performance-enhancing drugs at Angel Pharma, using these drugs to help his own kids achieve every kind of success, and then exporting the drugs to be used on kids in other countries, with the grand goal of spreading Angel-like perfection throughout the world.

Had my father really been a morally driven, visionary genius with a superior intellect? Or had he been a crass capitalist exploiting his own children for profit?

Was he courageous or shameless?

I thought I knew the answer.

My father was both.

"No. You have it, sweetheart."

My mother looked up at her husband, wearing a brave smile that tore at my heart. She said, "Thank you, Malcolm. I'll love you forever."

I turned away then. I knew it was where my father nodded and hugged my mother even harder. They were entwined when the seizures started.

I choked out, "Turn it off, Harry."

Tears were streaming down both of our faces.

"I'm sorry," said Sergeant Caputo. He reached out and touched my arm. "I'm very sorry for your loss."

# CONFESSION

*It probably won't surprise you* to hear me say that watching Nate Crosby's illicit video made me cry, longer and harder than I ever have in my life. But it might surprise you to hear me say that I wasn't crying because seeing my parents' death was so horrible.

I was crying because it was beautiful.

That was real, normal love—right here in the house of Angels. A man who couldn't bear the idea of living on this planet without the woman he married and had committed his life to. A woman despairing because she was dying and didn't have enough time to make everything right for her family. A woman crushed when she saw that the man she loved was taking his own life, too.

Okay, so maybe it wasn't exactly "normal." But it was the

most tangible proof I'd ever had that they loved each other so much.

*They loved each other. Malcolm and Maud loved each other.*

In their deaths, Malcolm and Maud had finally succumbed to their most basic emotions. Love. Fear of death. Fear of life without the one you cherish.

Witnessing their ultimate sacrifice had somehow given me the most valuable lesson of all. Now I knew I couldn't wait until the brink of death to finally be real and true to myself.

Their own Big Chop was going to save me.

# 84

*I'm not sure I could have* faced preparing a eulogy without seeing that video. As painful as it was, it gave me strength. If Malcolm and Maud truly believed we could do anything in life, even without them, I believed I could deliver this speech.

And I would not be a robot.

The press dogged us when we left the Dakota to attend the service, ran after us on the street, got right in our faces. It didn't matter to them that we were orphans. It didn't matter that we had been cleared of killing our parents.

As you might expect by now, the press was at its obnoxious worst. I hated them. They wanted interviews. They wanted drama. They wanted news. But we weren't going to give it to them. We kept where we were going secret so the press couldn't follow us.

Philippe was one of the very few friends invited to the extremely small, very private service at a funeral home on Eighty-third and Columbus. Despite how powerful and influential Malcolm and Maud were—or perhaps because of it—we didn't really know who their true allies and supporters were, so we decided to keep the invitation list to the very closest and oldest family and friends. I actually think our parents would have been proud of us—for trusting no one.

Philippe took the three of us aside before the service began and, without ceremony, delivered some information that forever rocked our worlds.

"Your mother had pancreatic cancer," Phil said. "Stage four. She didn't learn about it until it was too late for treatment. And this kind of cancer . . . There's no cure."

Although his explanations were clear, my mind was foggy. Not because I'd stopped taking the pills, but because I was oversaturated with feelings. I wasn't sure I was hearing him correctly.

"She was *dying*?" I'd deduced on some deeper level that illness was implied in the video of my parents' death, but it was stunning to hear the news nonetheless. "I just can't believe that, Phil. We would have seen something—medications, trips to the doctor...."

"She didn't want you children to know, Tandy. You know how important it was to your parents that you be strong, no matter what. I imagine Maud visited the hospital under the guise of work appointments, or while you were in school."

"It's not like we were ever allowed in their bathroom," Harry added. "She could have easily hidden her meds from us."

"As if anyone would have thought a bunch of pill bottles lying around was anything weird in our house," Hugo remarked, as astute as ever.

"She was a woman of many secrets," I murmured, remembering Samantha's words, vowing to find out more about what she knew, later.

Phil nodded. "I know how hard this is, but there's more I have to tell you. The SEC had filed a formal charge against Maud. She promoted Angel Pharma's stock and got all of her clients to buy in, but the company was crashing.

"She would have been indicted, for insider trading and for fraud. She wouldn't have lived long enough to be convicted, but she would have had to endure her last months in a hospital jail pending trial. She couldn't do that."

I pictured my mother chained to a rock. I saw the cancer tearing at her guts every day.

"And my father? What was he thinking?"

"Malcolm was going to file for bankruptcy," Philippe told me. "He didn't have a penny that wasn't borrowed. Everything your father owned was tied up in the company. But, most of all, he didn't want to live under any circumstances without your mother. What would his life have been like?"

Harry's eyes, so sad that morning, were now blazing. "You kept all of this from us? Even after our parents were dead? Even when this could have helped solve the case?"

"I only found out about your mother's illness yesterday, from the hospital—I was notified of some outstanding medical bills. Malcolm's plans to file for bankruptcy would have been addressed as we settled the estate. But the part about your father not wanting to live without your mother... well, he told me that himself. I only wish I had realized that he meant he was truly considering ending his life when hers ended. I would have tried to stop him."

I shook my head. I kept shaking it, a wordless *no, no, no*, until I became aware that Philippe had taken my hand and was saying my name.

"What will happen to us?" I asked him.

"I don't know. Your grandmother, Hilda Angel, didn't leave anything to your father, but she put what she had into a trust for any grandchildren who might be born later on. I don't think that the government will be able to take your inheritance from you, if there is one, but I won't have details until your parents' estates are settled."

At that moment, I hated my parents. I couldn't help it.

My parents had left us to pull our lives together without them. They had died penniless and with debts that would have to be satisfied. Would we even have a place to live?

And what's worse, Malcolm and Maud Angel had cheated and lied, and their selfishness had hurt a lot of people. They weren't just flawed, they were corrupt. And they corrupted their children because of their need for perfection. What could our parents have said in any "papers" that would comfort us now?

I went into the chapel desperately seeking good things to say about my parents. I tried to turn my mind back to the strength they'd given me.

I needed to bring healing words to my brothers. And to myself.

# 85

*The lights were low* in the simple little chapel. There were lilies in urns on either side of the podium, and the two caskets were below me—two dark wood coffins with sprays of white flowers lying across them. A large photo of my parents together stood on an easel to my left. They looked happy and optimistic in the picture, which had been taken twenty-five years ago.

Sadly, I wouldn't be able to lean on my big brother for support, since Matthew was still in jail and I wasn't even allowed to talk to him. So it was just Harry, Hugo, Samantha, and Philippe who looked up at me from the front row. They were counting on me to say the right things.

I didn't know if it was possible.

"Malcolm and Maud were good parents," I began. "They loved us in their own way."

My voice cracked and splintered. I tried to speak, but my broken little voice disappeared into the overwhelming sadness of my hollow words echoing in the small and nearly empty room.

I tried to rein in my grief and start again with sweeter memories in my mind.

I thought about the birthday cake my father had let me help him bake for Maud's birthday, and the way my mother had taught me how to dress and act. I remembered how effusive Maud had been when she described the great things I would do someday, including running the family business.

"They were tough on us, and, they held us to a high standard, because they loved us. They wanted us to do great things...."

"Because they *loved* us," Harry chimed in from the front row of the chapel. Tears were streaming down his face. "I know they did. They *had* to."

"They didn't tell us in actual words...."

"But they *did* love us," said Hugo, punching a fist into his other hand.

"They truly, truly loved you," said Samantha.

"They told me how much they loved you, many times," Phil said.

*Really?*

Where was all this certainty coming from? *I* wasn't sure. But it felt like the right thing to say. And I wanted so badly for it to be true. No matter what they'd done to me, I still loved them.

I think we all needed to believe that they loved us.

Suddenly, I was crying too hard to speak. I heard the creak of door hinges and looked up to see Uncle Peter entering at the front of the chapel. He looked like he'd been raised from the dead to attend this service.

I cleared my throat, dabbed at my nose with a tissue, and put up a hand to show that I had more to say.

I looked at my note cards so that I could read a quote. "Anne Frank wrote, 'How true Daddy's words were when he said: all children must look after their own upbringing. Parents can only give good advice or put them on the right paths, but the final forming of a person's character lies in their own hands.'

"This is how Malcolm and Maud felt about us," I said. "They trusted that we could shape our lives from this point on. That we could make our way."

Quoting what my mother had said only moments before she died just about killed me. I fell apart, blubbering and sobbing again.

Harry stood and spoke over my sobs. "Our parents

believed in working hard, and they taught us to earn everything we ever got. And now we finally understand that...that they did everything they did for us. It was *all* for us, right?" Harry looked around desperately. I nodded through my tears. He let out a huge sigh and covered his eyes with his hands. His shoulders shook and settled. He spoke again, adding, "Maud used to say, 'I'll sleep when I'm dead.' Sleep well now, Mother and Father." And he sat down.

Hugo shot to his feet and flung himself across Malcolm's coffin. He said, "Father, I forgive you for the biggest chop ever, ever, ever. I forgive *both* of you. Be good. No fighting. Buckle up and have a safe trip. We'll always love and miss you."

# EPILOGUE
# SHARKS

# 86

*Two days later,* we had all the windows open in our apartment in the Dakota.

Harry had turned up his music—not classical this time—so that it came over the intercom in every room, really loud. The charging drumbeat and the bright guitar riffs cleansed the air and made me almost want to dance.

Hugo was taking his baseball bat to the furniture in his room, which had been designed with some ordinary rich kid in mind—three big vintage toy cars with pedals, a make-believe rocket ship on a spring, and first-edition antique books that had never even been opened. All reminders of Angel wealth and perfection were quickly being decimated.

There was a lot of food on the dining room table: chips and dips and Ding Dongs—junk my parents would have forbidden. But Malcolm and Maud had left us to soldier on without them. And this laugh-out-loud time was a beautiful start. We felt like actual kids.

We were having a party. Our party. Just for us. We were finally grieving, in our own special way, as only Angels can.

I took a bottle of soda with me into my parents' room. Their valuables would be sold or auctioned off: the Aronstein flag, the South Sea pearls and the emerald ring, Mercurio and Robert, the Pegasus piano, the Pork Chair and the UFO light fixture.

Before it was too late, I wanted to go through my parents' less valuable things and find keepsakes for all of us.

I put on the jacket that had belonged to my mother by way of Madonna. I hoped I'd be able to keep it.

No, I was *definitely* going to keep it!

Harry came into the closet and sat down next to me.

"I've got Malcolm's watch," I said. "You want that?"

"Okay."

"I saved a couple of things for Matthew and Hugo. Pictures. The wedding rings."

"I'm the one who called the cops," Harry said.

"What do you mean?"

"That morning. Right after I found Malcolm and Maud dead. I thought one of us had done it. Still, I had to call the cops."

"Oh, *Harry*. Who was suspect number one on your list?"

"Well, sister dear, you'd just gotten a Big Chop."

I laughed really hard, then said, "For a while, I thought you did it. *You*."

We were still grinning at each other when a shadow fell over us.

I snapped my head around—a fear reflex, for sure. Virgil was standing there, absolutely huge in the doorway, looking down at us.

"I've got the car ready downstairs. You know the house rule, kids: I've got to move the vehicle in ten minutes."

"Let's move it," I said.

# 87

*The moon was high and full that night,* and the water in Shinnecock Bay was the same gorgeous indigo blue as the sky. The Ponquogue Bridge stretched out before us, spanning the bay, its gleaming white arc making me think of the leading edge of an angel's wing.

Harry, Hugo, Virgil, and I were grouped together at the foot of the bridge, listening to the soothing sound of waves slapping against the shore.

Then Hugo said, "Can we *go?*"

We took off our shoes and rolled up our trouser legs, each of us carrying a plastic bag with one of our sharks inside. Their green bioluminescence made the bags glow like lanterns. It was absolutely magical.

We stopped walking when the water was up to Hugo's chest and floated the bags so that the temperature of the water within would equalize with that of the bay.

It was completely quiet. Even Hugo was mesmerized into silence by the luminous, bobbing bags. But the sharks soon became restless. They banged into the sides of the bags and lashed their tails and frothed the water.

They knew what was coming.

Harry said, "I say that it's time."

We undid the rubber bands and opened the mouths of the bags. My heart seemed to expand as the sharks left their cocoons and swam into the open water.

Freedom. For real this time.

We all pointed and called to one another, clapping and cheering as the sharks circled, then formed a school and headed south toward the vast, open Atlantic.

A moment later their trail went dark, and suddenly the air and the water around me felt cold. I shivered and a million unanswered questions rose up and fluttered in my mind.

What had been the truth about my father and Tamara Gee? Had Matthew killed Tamara? Would he be convicted of murdering her? How would Harry and Hugo deal with their anger? With the drug withdrawal? What would we be like without the pills?

And of course there was a lot I would need to investigate about myself, too. I knew it wasn't a coincidence that the man suing my mother had the same last name as the boy I ran away with. James Rampling was Royal Rampling's son—that I knew. But what happened between the night I met James at the party and the day we escaped? Had James Rampling kidnapped me with ill intentions, or had he been my first genuine taste of love and freedom? And what on earth had happened to him after we were torn apart?

Would I ever see, touch, or hold him again? Did I even want to?

There are parts of those mysteries that I do remember, friend, fragments I'm still trying to work up the nerve to talk about. There are many more parts that I no longer remember, thanks to Dr. Keyes. But I know some places where I can start looking for answers.

As I stood in the bay thinking about the future, the framed letter from Gram Hilda came into my mind. She had left my parents a hundred dollars and a stinging slap. How had she provided for the grandchildren who had not yet been born when she died?

Would she leave us a Grande Gongo? Or would it be a Big Chop?

The night my parents were found dead, Uncle Peter said

to me, "After the reading of the will, we'll see what the future will bring to the Angel family."

Uncle Peter was wrong. Money was not going to influence our ability to succeed in the world.

The sharks had just amazed us. They had been confined for years and were now following their instincts, swimming together with strength and confidence out into the ocean.

It was a good sign.

In the last week, I had found my calling, what I was meant to do. I was going to be a detective. I might even have found mentors in Detectives Caputo and Hayes. I was surprisingly fond of them both, and I thought they felt the same way about me. They'd been unbelievably supportive and nice since they'd watched that video with us.

I could even see a possible business card in my mind:

TANDY ANGEL, DETECTIVE

MYSTERIES SOLVED. CASE CLOSED.

"What's so funny?" Harry asked me.

I looked up at my twin brother and said, "I was just thinking how much I love you guys."

At that, Hugo yelled, "Watch me!"

He put his arms out in front of him, dove under the water, and stroked toward the shore.

"Swim fast, die hard!" Harry hooted.

"We're both going to have to watch Hugo closely now. More than ever. And Matthew is going to need our help."

"It's a deal," Harry said. "I'm in."

My brothers and I had grown closer over the last few weeks. We were *still* growing, still *becoming*. I felt sure we would stick together, whatever happened, wherever the currents might carry us.

I really couldn't wait to see what we would do next.

And hey, it's been good talking to you. Really good.

# JAMES
# PATTERSON

**To find out more about James Patterson
and his bestselling books, go to
www.jamespatterson.co.uk**

We support

I'm proud to be working with the National Literacy Trust, a great charity that wants to inspire a love of reading.

If you loved this book, don't keep it to yourself. Recommend it to a friend or family member who might enjoy it too. Sharing reading together can be more rewarding than just doing it alone, and is a great way to help other people to read.

Reading is a great way to let your imagination run riot – picking up a book gives you the chance to escape to a whole new world and make of it what you wish. If you're not sure what else to read, start with the things you love. Whether that's bikes, spies, animals, bugs, football, aliens or anything else besides. There'll always be something out there for you.

Could you inspire others to get reading? If so, then you might make a great Reading Champion. Reading Champions is a reading scheme run by the National Literacy Trust. Ask your school to sign up today by visiting www.readingchampions.org.uk.

Happy Reading!

James Patterson